"Ethan," she whispered.

"That's impossible," he countered. "... won't stop just because we say so. Is there a rule that I shouldn't want you just because you're pregnant? Because I want you now more than ever."

"You can't say things like that." She was going for that scolding tone, but for some reason she ended up sounding breathless.

"Why? Because you're trying to lie to yourself and pretend you don't want me, too?"

Beneath that desire in his eyes lay humor. She couldn't lie to him and she shouldn't be lying to herself. She had to face every obstacle head-on.

"I just think..." Harper shook her head and stepped away. "I can't think when you're touching me and looking at me like that," she stated more firmly.

His lips quirked as he took another step toward her, then another until he'd backed her fully into the open ballroom. Without a word, he reached behind him and slid the doors closed, the smack of the wood echoing through the room.

* * *

California Secrets is the second book
in the Two Brothers duet.

Dear Reader,

I hope you loved Dane's story in *Montana Seduction*, which was set in the snowy mountains! Now I'm thrusting you onto a private tropical island for Ethan's story. While he may seem like a playboy at first, he has deep-rooted emotional scars that lead to all of his actions, I promise.

Those actions have consequences when he meets Harper. This headstrong heroine isn't interested in a relationship. She has her own agenda, but she can't resist Ethan or a heated fling. But when she ends up expecting his baby, they'll have to decide what's more important—their career goals or becoming a family.

I hope you love Ethan's story as much as I do. I truly believe he's one of those heroes who is misunderstood and it takes a special leading lady to "get" him.

Happy reading!

Jules

JULES BENNETT

—

CALIFORNIA SECRETS

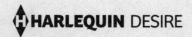

Recycling programs
for this product may
not exist in your area.

ISBN-13: 978-1-335-60388-3

California Secrets

Copyright © 2019 by Jules Bennett

HARLEQUIN®
www.Harlequin.com

Printed in U.S.A.

USA TODAY bestselling author **Jules Bennett** has published over sixty books and never tires of writing happy endings. Writing strong heroines and alpha heroes is Jules's favorite way to spend her workdays. Jules hosts weekly contests on her Facebook fan page and loves chatting with readers on Twitter, Facebook and via email through her website. Stay up-to-date by signing up for her newsletter at julesbennett.com.

Books by Jules Bennett

Harlequin Desire

The Rancher's Heirs

Twin Secrets
Claimed by the Rancher
Taming the Texan
A Texan for Christmas

Texas Cattleman's Club: Houston

Married in Name Only

Two Brothers

Montana Seduction

California Secrets

Visit her Author Profile page at Harlequin.com, or julesbennett.com, for more titles.

You can find Jules Bennett on Facebook, along with other Harlequin Desire authors, at Facebook.com/harlequindesireauthors!

To my sister, Angel.
You're always willing to drop your
workload to help me with mine.
Love you more than cake!

One

The red bikini never failed to arouse him…and the damn thing was just hanging there on the heated towel bar in his en suite.

When Harper Williams donned that collection of triangles and strings, he always enjoyed peeling the flimsy material from her curvy body. As much as he always wanted to tear it off, he enjoyed this sexy suit way too much to destroy it.

Ethan Michaels slid on a gray T-shirt and stepped back into the bedroom of his penthouse at Mirage. The adults-only resort was beyond luxurious and grand. In addition to all the amenities that made this five-star resort so sought out, the breathtaking property sat in the middle of Sunset Cove, a private island off the southern coast of California, making this resort a most magnificent destination.

While waiting out his time until he orchestrated an epic surprise reunion with his bastard of a stepfather, Ethan had started a fling with the owner of that tempting red bikini. He'd always been a sucker for red…and the lush body beneath didn't hurt, either.

The one-night stand had turned into nearly a month of passion and R-rated sleepovers. Even with the time that had passed, he and Harper had kept things casual, simple—just the way he preferred his temporary arrangements, and she seemed more than okay with how their fling was going.

Ethan had no clue what brought Harper as a single guest to Mirage—and he had no intention of asking. She'd been alone like him, and they'd just gravitated toward each other, as most people who came to the adults-only resort were couples.

He and Harper had fallen into a perfect routine of meeting in his room for dinner in the evening. He'd always make sure the chef prepared something special just for them and the waitstaff always accommodated every need—Ethan would remember each loyal employee when he took the resort back into his name.

There was never a set time for Harper showing up in the evening, but Ethan always made sure something was ready for her. During the day, though, they did their own thing and went their own ways. Occasionally he'd see her on the beach and take her a drink, but they never so much as touched outside his penthouse.

Watching her parade around on the beach seemed to be the ultimate foreplay.

But he couldn't get too distracted—he still had a job to do, a vendetta to secure. His time here wasn't all about play. Harper was just an enjoyable by-product. He didn't care one bit that she seemed to be using him to pass her time, as well. He did wonder what she was biding her time for, but again, he didn't want to pry, because anything personal was out of the question.

All it would take would be one quick message to his assistant to have any answer he wanted about Harper, but that would imply that he wanted to know her beyond the bedroom. Some may call him cold, and they might be right, but Ethan had his reasons for the distance, and they were nobody else's concern.

Besides, he never started a fling if the woman wasn't on board for something casual and fun or if he thought for a second she was husband shopping. He'd never lead a woman on or pretend he could offer anything more than his body and a small portion of his time.

So, while some may think he was a coldhearted

bastard, the only person who was hurt at the end of the day was himself. It was that pain that kept him focused on why he sought revenge, why vindication was so important. Using women was never his plan, but using his own body was.

Ethan grabbed his cell from the nightstand and checked his emails as he stepped onto the balcony. That fresh salt water and the ocean breeze never got old. He was meant for the beach, while his twin brother, Dane, was meant for the mountains. They were so alike, yet so different.

Nothing too pressing on the email front, so Ethan sent a text to his investigator to make sure the timeline for Robert Anderson's arrival was still correct. His dear ol' stepfather had been due at Mirage three weeks ago, but for some reason or another—likely illegal—the man was running very late. People like Robert flittered around from one spot to the next without a real plan or too much of a schedule.

But Ethan was patient. He'd waited nearly twenty years to get retribution…a few more days wouldn't matter.

He pocketed his phone and glanced down to the beach. White canopies draped over the two-person cabanas. Staff roamed around with trays of drinks. The calming water rolled up against the shoreline, only to roll back out again. Yeah, he could easily stay right here and wait on Robert because passing his time at a posh luxury resort while enjoying passionate nights with Harper was sure as hell better than anything else he could be doing for work or otherwise. He used his days to maintain and work on growing his night clubs across the country, and he couldn't think of a better temporary office to work from.

Mirage—the beautiful resort his mother had created, which had been wrenched away from her sons after her death—was always meant to be his. This place felt like home, and soon, so very soon, he'd be in charge just like his mother had always intended.

With the twentieth anniversary of her death approaching, Ethan knew it was well past time to make Lara Anderson's dream a reality. Sticking Robert Anderson in some hellhole where he belonged would just be icing on the proverbial cake.

As Ethan turned back toward the living area, his cell vibrated in his pocket. He pulled it out to see Harper's name light up the screen.

Strange. They never texted or called. They kept this arrangement strictly superficial.

Where are you?

He hesitated but ultimately replied that he was in his penthouse. She'd only been gone from his bed a few hours. Since she'd left, he'd gotten in a full workout and managed to touch base with each of his managers for his nightclubs across the country.

He was in the middle of branching out globally and hoped a deal in France would close soon.

Time zones were often a bitch to work around, but he had a dedicated staff and couldn't run his company without such trusted members. Ethan demanded loyalty and, in turn, compensated his crew nicely.

He already had a master plan of who he'd bring on to Mirage to help with a smooth transition, though he fully intended on keeping the bulk of the resort's staff, so long as they proved themselves worthy. He expected nothing but the best, especially where his mother's legacy was concerned.

Ethan glanced back to his phone again, but Harper hadn't replied. He had no clue what she wanted, but he needed to touch base with his brother. They might have drifted apart when their mother died, they might have dealt with her death in their own ways and closed out the world and each other, but Dane was all Ethan had left. No matter their past grief, Ethan always knew he could count on his twin.

They'd forged together to make a solid plan in reclaiming their mother's pair of properties. Dane had acquired his resort in the mountains of Montana—now it was Ethan's turn.

Mirage in Montana had been seized by Robert, but with a bad gambling move, he'd lost the place. Dane had gone in with a plan of charming the new owner's daughter. He'd succeeded in acquiring the property, but somehow, he'd managed to fall in love and was planning a wedding.

Ethan would just take the property. Hold the wife.

He'd just pulled up Dane's texts when the penthouse elevator whooshed open. Ethan shifted his focus from the phone to Harper.

As much as he appreciated her in, and out, of that red bikini, he had to admit those lush curves were killer in her strapless emerald green sundress. All that dark skin on display…damn, he couldn't wait until tonight. Maybe she'd still have that dress on, because that thing sure as hell would provide easy access.

Her jet-black curls spiraled down her back with random strands draped over her shoulders. There was nothing about this woman he didn't find sexy and appealing. Had she come here because she couldn't wait for tonight?

No. That wasn't desire staring back at him. There was a look in her rich brown eyes that had him stilling, his heart clenching…not in a good way. She crossed the spacious suite, her wide gaze never wavering from his. The only sign that she was nervous or upset was the way she toyed with the delicate gold bracelet she always wore.

"What happened?" he asked, knowing she wouldn't be here with that panicked look in her eyes nor would she have texted him unless something was wrong.

"We have to talk."

Ethan let those words sink in before he let out a bark of laughter. "That sounds like the precursor to a breakup."

Which didn't make sense, considering they weren't an actual couple. There was nothing to break up.

Her worried look didn't even crack. "That's not why I'm here."

"Then what has you looking like your world has come to an end?"

Harper took in a deep breath, and for the first time since they'd met a month ago, she didn't seem like the confident, poised woman he'd come to know.

"I'm pregnant."

Saying those two words out loud didn't make this situation seem any more real or any less terrifying. Since taking the test this morning, she'd been in a fog, wondering how to tell Ethan, worried how he'd react, scared for her own future and how she'd provide a child with a stable home. But Harper had never backed down from a problem or a confrontation. She'd overcome so much heartache and tragedy, she couldn't look at this like a mistake or a setback.

Harper firmly believed everything happened for

a reason…even if she didn't understand and the timing was less than ideal.

Her entire life since Ethan approached her on the beach had been a series of firsts—the red bikini, the one-night stand, the continuation of that one night into an ongoing fling with a virtual stranger, the shower sex, the balcony sex in the middle of the night and now the two blue lines.

She'd had one serious relationship, but that had ended just before her sister died. Harper wasn't looking for any other commitment that would inevitably bring on more pain. But the fear of this situation settled heavy between them.

"Say something," she demanded after the yawning silence only added to her ever growing worry.

Ethan's bright eyes locked onto her. "You're serious."

Harper let out a mock laugh. "Do you think this is something I'd joke about?"

After another moment of awkward, tension-filled silence, Ethan muttered a curse and shook his head.

"No, but I don't know what to think." He raked a hand through his messy hair before shifting his attention back to her. "I won't ask how you know it's mine. I may not know much about you, but I know you haven't shared anyone else's bed."

"You're the first man I've been with in nearly a year."

Harper smoothed a hand over her queasy belly.

She was more nervous about this conversation than she was nauseated from the pregnancy. But she hadn't been with a man in so long, which would explain part of the reason why she'd found Ethan so charming and irresistible. The other reason was because she was still trying to find her footing with her late sister's company, and Harper had used sex with Ethan as a much-needed means of escape.

She also kept hearing her sister's nagging in the back of her mind. Her fun-loving, life-of-the-party sister who always had encouraged Harper to step out of her comfort zone. Coming to this resort alone, wearing that bikini in a size fourteen, faking a confidence she didn't feel…all of these things were firsts for her.

"I didn't want to keep this from you," she went on, then paced to the double doors leading to the balcony. "I just found out this morning. I realize we barely know each other, but I'm not the type of person to lie or mislead anyone."

Life was too short, her goals too big to play games with anyone. She'd seen him, wondered what a fling would be like since she'd never had one, then decided to take charge of her life and seize the moment. She'd been trying to do more living in the moment since Carmen passed.

She'd brought the red bikini with her because her sister had always accused her of being too boring, too vanilla, and Harper had wanted to put herself out there with a bold confidence.

Now look where that landed her.

"You seem calm."

Harper glanced over her shoulder and collected her thoughts. "Calm? I'm scared to death, I'm stunned, I'm worried how I'll juggle it all. Getting hysterical won't change a thing or help me sort out these feelings. So, maybe I am calm, but it's not because I'm comfortable, it's because I'm shocked."

Those piercing eyes usually held so much desire and passion, but now...

Harper turned her attention back to the breathtaking view of the turquoise water and white sand. She didn't want to witness his worry, his doubts... She had her own to deal with. This was the last thing she wanted to confront him about, but he deserved to know. This temporary fling had now resulted in a lifetime connection to Ethan Michaels. As if she didn't have enough going on in her life already.

Coming to Mirage had been the first step she'd taken in moving her and her sister's design business into the next phase. Harper had every intention of making Two Sisters Design the go-to for every business, every home owner, everyone who wanted a change in their office or house or hotel.

Carmen had always had a grand vision of their business. Harper had been reluctant at first when

Carmen asked for her help, worried she wouldn't measure up to her sister's amazing talents, despite Carmen's high praise on small projects.

But after her sister was killed in a robbery six months ago, Harper knew she had to step up and take over. It's what her sister would've wanted. Carmen would've had faith in Harper. Harper just needed to have faith in herself…which was how she landed at Mirage.

She'd decided to start here because her father owned the adults-only resort. He wanted to do an overhaul and, though she'd first met the man when she was twenty, she was trying to have a relationship with him. Trying…and somewhat succeeding.

Robert Anderson was a man who traveled and worked all over the world. Seemed business was more important to him than family, but what did she expect? He hadn't even known she'd existed for two decades, so she shouldn't have expected him to jump into the role of doting daddy. Yet she had expected just that.

Her sister was all she'd truly had in life, and now that she was gone, Harper craved any semblance of family. Her free-spirited mother gallivanting around the globe didn't count.

Harper wasn't sure what all her father did for a living, but she knew he was in real estate. And he'd been willing to give her a chance with one of his most prestigious properties. Having Mirage in her portfolio would seriously help boost her business.

And she would carry out her duties to prove to her father, to herself and to her sister that she was capable...despite starting a family much sooner than she'd ever planned.

"What's going through your mind?"

Ethan's sincere question filled the room, and she turned to face him. She couldn't help but laugh as she fiddled with the gold bracelet at her wrist.

"I have no idea," she told him. "I have so many thoughts, but I do want you to know that I don't expect anything from you. I won't make you do anything you're not ready for. I'm a big girl—I can handle anything thrown at me."

Wow. Her little speech sounded strong, though she felt anything but. Yet, despite her anxiety, she couldn't let the fear win, because that's not what Carmen would've wanted. One tragic event after another had made her steely when it came to pain and reactions, but she wasn't about to let Ethan into her past, into her mind and all the reasons why she wasn't flipping out right now.

"Listen," she began, shoving her wayward curls over her shoulders. "This is a lot to think about. We'll just take some time to process and then talk later. I know we haven't gotten too personal with our information, but I will be here for at least another month, probably longer. And even then, I'll be coming and going quite a bit."

She'd never told him her reason for being here. Their physical relationship left no room for small talk or the get-to-know-you phase. Everything would change now. They'd have to dig into each other's lives, because now they were bonded forever.

When Ethan continued to stare at her across the room, Harper figured she should go and leave him alone with his thoughts. She wasn't sure what to say right now. Her purpose for coming to his room had been to tell him the truth, but she hadn't thought much beyond that.

Harper pulled in a shaky breath and started across the penthouse. The moment she stepped by him, Ethan's arm snaked out and caught her around the waist, his hand curling around her arm. Sliding his thumb over the inside of her elbow, he stopped her with that one simple, arousing gesture.

Her body responded, just as it always did to his tantalizing touch and heavy-lidded stare. Ethan Michaels was a potent man, and now she had to figure out how to shift from looking at him as a fling to seeing him as the father of her child...which wasn't going to be easy, considering she didn't know basic things like his middle name or even where he was from.

"You're not leaving," he told her. "We may not

figure out all the answers now, but I know one thing for certain."

Why did his tone sound like a promising threat?

Ethan's eyes held her as breath caught in her throat. "You're not doing this alone. I *will* be part of this baby's life…and yours."

Two

Ethan might not know how to handle this situation, but he sure as hell knew he wasn't about to walk away from responsibility. This was a child... *his* child. His family life may be uncertain and in shreds, but deep down, at the end of the day, family mattered more to him than anything in this world.

Wasn't that why he was here to begin with? Every action he'd taken over the past twenty years had led him to this moment, all for the sake of his late mother and her wishes.

No matter what might come of him and Harper, that child was his future, and he would provide and be part of his or her life.

"I don't want a relationship just because I'm pregnant," she stated with a defiant tilt of her chin.

Ethan released her arm but didn't back away. She was quite adamant about this whole casual, un- committed relationship status, which was perfectly fine with him, but each time it had been mentioned or hinted at, Harper had a flash of hurt in her eyes.

Who had hurt her? What had she gone through to bring her to this point? More importantly, why did he care to make it his business? He'd known about this baby for all of five minutes, and already his mind was playing with him. He had his own past hurts to focus on. Not that he wanted Harper to be in pain—he'd never want that—but he couldn't afford to get swept into her world and risk losing sight of his goals.

"I never said anything about a relationship," he countered. "But we're bonded together whether we like it or not."

Beneath that steely look in her dark eyes there was a hint of vulnerability and fear. She wasn't quite as calm as she led him to believe, but he'd be more worried if she wasn't scared. Hell, he was ter- rified, but there was nothing that would pull him away from his child or the woman carrying it.

His mother had been a hardworking, single mom. Ethan couldn't ignore the parallels here.

He would have Robert Anderson out of the pic- ture and this resort back in his possession before his baby was born. Timing and persistence were everything right now.

"How long are you staying?" she asked. "We probably should dig a little deeper into each other since, well…"

She was more than welcome to go ahead and dig, but he would only feed her enough information to pacify her curiosities until he had his personal life all straightened out. No need to involve her in his family affair, which he was quite certain would get messy.

"I have no set plans." Partial truth, but all he was willing to give. "I'm here for as long as I want to be."

Harper's brows drew in. "You're so vague. Please tell me you're not married or running from the law."

Ethan laughed. "I'm not running from the law, and isn't it a little late to ask about a wife?"

"I assumed you didn't have one before we hooked up, but now I feel I should know the truth."

Ethan shook his head. "No wife, no girlfriend. I have a twin brother in Montana, and that's all the family I have. Well, he's getting married soon, so I guess I'll have a sister."

Harper's gaze darted down to her clasped hands, and he thought he saw that flash of hurt again, but maybe not. Maybe he just couldn't read her well enough quite yet. He knew exactly how to read her in the bedroom, but now, well…this was completely new territory. Trying to get a bead on women emotionally had always been foreign to him.

"What about you?" he asked.

Harper shifted her attention back to him. "I have a father that I met when I was twenty. My mother is a little eccentric and floats from one spot on the globe to the next. I'm not sure what hemisphere she's in half the time. I had a sister, but she passed away six months ago. She was…everything to me. I'm still trying to figure out how to do life without her."

Well, damn. Not what he thought she'd say. He'd pegged her for someone with several siblings, doting parents that all gathered around a big table for each holiday. He figured she was here as a loner to get away and have some time for herself.

But instead, she was alone. Like him.

Oh, he had Dane, but since their mother's death, nothing had been the same. For nearly twenty years, an invisible wedge had separated them, and Ethan was hoping that by getting their mother's resorts back, maybe they'd find closure and get back that relationship they'd once had.

So, his twin was getting a wife and Ethan was getting a child. Not at all what he'd envisioned when they'd started this journey.

"Sounds like we have something in common besides physical attraction," he told her. "Loss of family is… It's rough."

Harper tucked a dark curl behind her ear and nodded. "I'm keeping this baby."

She laid claim like she dared him to argue. He had to admire a woman who wasn't afraid to say exactly what she wanted and made no apologies about it.

"I assumed," Ethan replied. "If you hadn't wanted to, I would have tried to change your mind. Family is everything to me."

Harper pursed her lips then blew out a sigh. She stepped back from him and headed toward the patio doors once again, only this time she opened them and stepped on out into the sunshine. Ethan followed her, having no clue what to say or do. For the first time in his life, his confidence, his control slipped.

No, that wasn't true. His control had slipped when his mother died and Robert stole everything from him and Dane. Ethan had vowed to never feel helpless again—which was why he was taking this revenge head-on.

Ethan moved in beside Harper and rested his arm on the railing. The ocean breeze lifted her curls from her shoulders and sent them dancing in the wind. His body responded, immediately recalling how those strands glided over his bare skin.

Damn it. He shouldn't be lusting after her now, but, well…he couldn't help himself. Knowing she was carrying his child made her even sexier, and he hadn't thought that was possible.

"It's clear that you want to be involved, but I need you to know that I really don't expect you to be there every minute."

"Duly noted."

She turned her attention to him for a brief moment, but then she glanced back to the ocean. "So what now?"

"I'll bring a doctor to the resort to make sure you and the baby are healthy." Damn. He was a selfish idiot. He hadn't even asked the obvious question. "Are you feeling okay?"

Harper nodded. "Tired and nervous, but that's all."

"Don't worry. I'm going to take care of you both. I'll have the doctor here by the end of the day," he stated.

Harper laughed as she jerked her gaze back to him. "Do people normally just jump when you snap your fingers?"

"Yes."

Shaking her head, she turned away from him and crossed to the chaise. "Well, I have my own doctor, and I'll call her to see what to do."

She took a seat and stretched out, lacing her fingers over her abdomen. He immediately envisioned her in a few months with their child growing. Emotions flooded him—anticipation, worry, uncertainty, excitement.

"I meant what about us now?" she asked. "We're not exactly a couple, and this certainly changes things between us."

"Nothing about this attraction has changed," he replied.

Ethan had to force himself to remain still, to not cross the balcony and take a seat on the chaise and pull her into his lap. They had never been alone this long without touching. The ache inside him grew with each passing minute, but they both needed to process this life-altering moment, and Harper needed space. Hell, so did he, but he still wanted to use sex as a distraction...just like he'd always done.

Only this time that default mode wasn't going to be the best option. He had to care, had to put himself out there, at least a little, because he was going to be a father.

The idea nearly had his weak knees buckling. What did he know about parenting? His mother had been a saint putting up with twin boys, but she'd suffered a fatal stroke when they'd been teens. The only father figure he'd had around was Robert Anderson, and that had just been for a handful of years and had ended when the bastard stole everything from Dane and Ethan. So this was going to be one area he had to learn all on his own...a vulnerable spot to find himself in.

Harper swung her legs over the side of the chaise and came to her feet.

"Listen, I have some things I need to do today," she told him. "We both should take some time to process, and I will contact my own doctor."

"I will—"

Harper held up her hands. "I don't deal well with anyone trying to control me—that's going to be the first personal thing about me you need to understand. I can take care of getting my own health care. I promise not to leave you out."

Ethan didn't like it, but he understood her need to be in charge of her own body. Now he didn't stop himself from crossing the patio. He did, however, use all his willpower to prevent himself from reaching for her.

"Come back tonight," he told her. "Eight. I'll have dinner ready."

Her dark eyes leveled his. "You don't seriously want to keep this up."

Ethan took another step until their bodies lined up perfectly, then he framed her face with his hands and covered her lips with his. She arched against him and let out a little moan, the same moan that always drove him out of his mind. This time was no different.

Just as quickly as he'd started the kiss, Ethan released her and took a step back.

"I'll see you at eight."

Ethan moved back into the penthouse and headed toward the bedroom. As dramatic exits went, that wasn't the best. But, considering they were in his suite, he couldn't exactly leave.

He waited until he heard the elevator chime her departure before he sank onto the edge of the bed. What the hell had he gotten himself into?

He'd always prided himself on keeping all emotions and people out. That was how he'd lived for the last twenty years, but he was going to have a hell of a time continuing on that path. Harper needed him, and so did their child. That slap of reality had Ethan more afraid than anything. Was he even capable of opening up? Could he be what a child even needed?

Money was one thing—he had plenty of that and could offer everything Harper and a child could ever want. But he wasn't going to be a hands-off dad…he just had no clue how to open his heart just enough for his baby and not get hurt.

After being shut down for so long, Ethan wondered if any of this was even possible.

Three

Harper clutched the notepad and pen as she circled the open ballroom once more. She would've already had all the last-minute notes she needed had her mind not been preoccupied volleying back and forth between redecorating Mirage and decorating a nursery.

Focus.

She had to remain true to her sister's dream and to this job. Yes, her life had taken a complete twist from what she'd planned, but she wasn't going to get off course. She had a job to do, and what type of mother would she be if she just gave up on her commitments whenever life got difficult or scary?

There. See? She was already thinking like a parent...not that she knew much about that role. The closest thing she'd had, her one and only life support, Carmen, had been taken much too soon. Harper would give anything to have her sister/parent/best friend here to offer advice or a hug. Harper could definitely use a consoling hug right about now.

Tears pricked her eyes, and she cursed as she blinked them away. Getting upset wouldn't change a thing, which was why she needed to focus and stay on track.

Harper jotted down a few more last-minute notes as she slowly made her way around the open space once again. This room was currently closed off from the rest of the resort. From what Harper could gather, when Mirage first opened, there had been quite a few extravagant dances and receptions here. She wanted to bring this room back to life and compete with the newer resorts that had opened recently.

The resort was beautiful; the location demanded nothing less. But there were areas that had been overlooked and neglected for a few years, and she was overly excited, if a bit nervous, to revamp the entire place and polish those hidden gems back to a new sparkle.

She'd already done all of her designs and had everything ready to go. But the nervous worker inside her wouldn't let her rest. She wanted to look at each room, making sure there were things she hadn't forgotten.

This would undoubtedly be the most pivotal project she may ever take on. Perfect timing considering she was also taking on the most important role of her life…mother.

Harper glanced to her notes and realized in all her wanderings over the past couple of hours, she'd managed to doodle a baby rattle on the paper.

She'd always been one to leave random drawings on her work, but she truly had no idea she'd done this on her sketches and notes about the ballroom.

Good thing she was the only one who would see these, right?

Just as Harper started to leave the grand ballroom, her cell vibrated in her dress pocket. With her free hand, she pulled it out and stared at the text from her doctor's office confirming her appointment.

She'd make a quick day trip to LA and be back here and on the job, hopefully before her father arrived. She really wished he'd get here, because there was only so much she could do without getting his approval. Oh, she'd love to have free rein, but he wanted to give one final okay to everything before she was let loose with the funding to start tearing up all the old to replace with new.

Sliding the cell back in her pocket, Harper made

a mental note to tell Ethan about the appointment when she met up with him later. And that was just absurd. Going back to his penthouse for dinner like they'd been doing, like they were just going to continue this fling as if nothing had changed.

Talk. That's all they could do tonight. There would be no sex. In fact, she'd find the ugliest thing she'd packed and wear it. Granny panties, too. Nothing sexy at all was going into that penthouse suite.

Actually, Harper should probably tell him they'd have dinner in one of the main restaurants. That would be best all around. They needed to curtail their desires. They'd had sex—amazing, toe-curling sex—but now it was time to move on and figure out what was best for all three of them.

First, she needed to learn more about the man. How cliché could she be? Meet a man, have a fling and still know nothing about him. Of course, she knew that if her sister was here, Carmen would likely buy Harper a drink and toast to the fact Harper had finally let loose and had a good time… then she'd promptly follow that up with some very real advice on how to embrace this new role of becoming a mother.

Of the two sisters, Harper had definitely been the more responsible, the more structured one. Carmen had taken after their mother with a little more of a free-bird mentality. Harper had never let loose…ever. She'd been so structured—until she came here.

But now more than ever, she'd need that structured mind-set to get through the project and her pregnancy. She needed a timeline and some type of plan for the future. Raising a baby while trying to grow a business would be a challenge, she had no doubt. But she wasn't going to worry about that now. Millions of women worked and raised children. Harper had no doubt she could and would do just fine.

Harper slid open the door to the hallway and jumped.

"Ethan," she gasped. "What are you doing here? This area is closed off to guests."

If his wide eyes were any indication, he was just as surprised to see her.

"So why are you here?" he countered.

Harper chewed the inside of her cheek and considered how much to share. He'd find out everything at some point anyway, right? They'd well surpassed the fling stage.

"I was actually hired to revamp this resort," she confessed. "That's why I've been here so long—and will be for a while longer. I need to be part of each step and oversee the progress."

Ethan stared at her for another moment, his brows drawn in as if trying to figure something out. Silence settled between them, and she wondered what could be so interesting about what she'd just said.

"So you're an interior designer?" he asked.

"By default," she half joked. "My sister was the truly brilliant designer, but she always said I had a good eye. She opened Two Sisters Design a year ago and begged me to join her, so I did. And then... Well, you know she passed, so here I am."

Ethan remained silent as he shoved his hands in his pockets and rocked back on his heels. The quiet air seemed to crackle around them, and she hated this awkwardness that settled between them.

"And that's enough of my backstory for now."

She hated the tension that had slid between them. She had no clue how to act or what to say around him, which seemed rather odd considering they'd spent nearly every night together over the past month. Flings were messy, they were confusing, they were...

Harper mentally gave herself a slap in the face to wake up. She wasn't having a fling anymore. She was having a baby with a man she barely knew. Which raised the question of his presence here now. Had he followed her?

"What are you doing here?" she asked again.

Ethan shrugged. "Just wandering around."

"This whole area is closed off." The manager knew who she was and allowed her access to any part of the resort. "How did you get in here at all? The door to this whole portion is coded."

"Code?" he asked with a shake of his head. "The door was wide-open when I came through. I wasn't aware it was closed off."

Harper couldn't tell if he was lying or if the door had in fact been left open. He had no reason to lie that she knew of, but she was sure she hadn't left the door open. Something was off, but she couldn't exactly say if it was Ethan or not.

"So, you're revamping the entire resort?" he asked, glancing over her shoulder into the open ballroom. "That seems like quite the undertaking for one person."

"I'm up for the challenge. Besides, I have a team that will come in and do the physical work."

No need to tell him this was her first solo gig. She couldn't treat this as a rookie project. Now more than ever, Two Sisters needed her entire focus.

Ethan took a step toward her, and that focus tilted. How could a man wearing a pair of well-worn jeans and a T-shirt be so damn attractive? Oh, yeah. Because she knew every inch of muscle tone that lay beneath those clothes.

He slid the back of his knuckles across her cheek. Harper's breath caught in her throat as she closed her eyes and relished in his touch. When would she get over this? Would his touch always make her body tremble, her head foggy, her belly tingle?

"Ethan," she whispered as she focused back on his hungry gaze. "We need to stop this."

"That's impossible," he countered, bringing his other hand up and framing her face. "The attraction won't stop just because we say so. Is there a rule that I shouldn't want you just because you're pregnant? Because I want you now more than ever."

More than ever. In their month-long fling, she'd come to crave him more than anything, so she understood his need. They matched each other so perfectly in the bedroom. Never before had she experienced anything like Ethan Michaels…and the man was quite an experience.

"You can't say things like that." She was going for a scolding tone, but for reasons she ended up sounding breathless.

"Why? Because you're trying to lie to yourself and pretend you don't want me, too?"

She couldn't lie to him, and she shouldn't be lying to herself. She had to face every obstacle head-on.

"I just think…"

Harper shook her head and stepped away.

"I *can't* think when you're touching me and looking at me like that," she stated more firmly.

His lips quirked as he took another step toward her, then another until he'd backed her fully into the open ballroom. Without a word, he reached behind him and slid the doors closed, the smack of the wood echoing through the room.

"You love every second of my touching and looking."

That throaty tone sent shivers through her.

"We're having a baby," she stressed, as if he didn't already know. "You said yourself that changes things between us."

"It changes the timeline," he stated, reaching for a curl and wrapping it around his finger. "It means we'll be part of each other's lives forever. But it sure as hell doesn't change anything else."

Harper tipped her head and stared up into those bright eyes. She could get lost in them, and on several nights, she'd done just that. There was something so powerful and mysterious about Ethan that she'd never been able to put her finger on. She'd wondered what brought him here, what kept him here, and now she really wanted to satisfy her curiosity.

Before she could dig deeper into this man who'd swept into her world and turned it upside down, he eased down and captured her lips. Ethan slid one hand through her hair and the other hand over the small of her back, pressing her body into his.

The response was instantaneous as the familiar tingle swept through her. Harper gripped his biceps, just trying to hold on to some sort of stability. This kiss was no different than the others. Every one created an arousing sensation that slithered from her head to her toes and made her knees weak.

Ethan spun them until her back came in contact with the wall. Wedged between two rock-hard surfaces, Harper arched against Ethan's chest as his lips traveled from her mouth down the column of her throat. She tipped her head to the side, giving him more room to work even as a niggling voice in the back of her head kept telling her all the reasons she shouldn't be doing this.

Harper really wished that voice would shut up and just let her enjoy the moment. Ethan's hands bustled up the skirt of her maxidress. That voice grew louder, telling her to put an end to the madness.

"Need you now," he murmured against her ear. The warmth from his breath sent even more shivers coursing through her.

There was a clatter as something fell to the floor and tapped the side of her foot. She ignored it.

Then ringing sounded through the room. She ignored that, too, because Ethan's talented fingertips cruised along the edge of her panty line and silently promised delicious things.

The annoying ring persisted.

Her cell.

"Wait." Harper pressed her hands to Ethan's chest. "My phone."

"Leave it," he demanded.

She pressed a bit more until he muttered a curse and took a step back. Her dress fell back around her legs and she tapped her pockets, frantically searching for her cell before realizing it had fallen to the floor. Harper grabbed the phone and turned away from Ethan before she managed to control her shaky hands enough to look at the screen.

Of all times for this call.

"I have to take this," she stated over her shoulder.

Without another word, she walked toward the wall of windows and accepted the call. Her hands shook and her body still hadn't caught up with the fact there was nothing fabulous on the verge of happening right this minute.

"Hey," she answered, trying to catch her breath. "I've been wondering when I'd hear from you."

"I've been a bit busy," her father said. "But I just boarded my jet and wanted to touch base. My assistant mentioned you wanted to change some things from the original design."

"I do. In fact, I sent not only the new ideas but a new budget."

All correspondence for the renovations was supposed to go through her father's second in command. She didn't ask why—Harper was just glad to have the job.

"Good work," he praised. "I'll take a look at everything, but I trust your decisions. I'll have my assistant get with you about the new materials so you will be ready when your crew arrives. She mentioned next week sometime?"

"That's right," Harper confirmed. "I can't wait for you to see my vision."

Harper glanced over her shoulder, not surprised to see Ethan staring back at her. She turned her focus back toward the window.

"And when are you coming exactly?" she asked.

"Soon," he promised. "But I want you to go ahead and get started. Bring in however many people you need, and I'll okay the budget. I know I wanted to approve everything, but I simply don't have the time and I believe you'll do right by my resort."

A thrill shot through her at the idea of starting to bring her vision to life in a matter of days. After months of waiting, wondering if she could live up to her sister's vision and hopes, now was Harper's chance to prove to everyone, especially herself, that she was worthy of this position her sister had trusted her with.

"Everything else going smoothly?" he asked. "I trust your upgraded suite and the staff are nothing short of perfection."

"Oh, yeah. Everything is fine."

I'm just pregnant by a virtual stranger from a heated fling, but that shouldn't hinder my ability to choose paint swatches and lighting fixtures.

"I can't wait to see you," she said, smiling and

wanting happiness and excitement to come through in her tone. "Hopefully soon."

"Hopefully," he repeated in a monotone voice. "I have to run. My assistant will be in touch."

He disconnected the call, and a little twinge of sadness clipped her heart. He didn't seem excited to actually see her, only concerned with the renovations. Granted, he'd gone over two decades without having a child, so she had to cut him some slack. Carmen had a different father and had actually had a relationship with him.

But Harper had been in Robert's life for several years now, and he still hadn't fully embraced fatherhood like she'd hoped.

Especially now, she wished he'd be a little more… well, just a little more. Anything would give her hope they might eventually get to a loving relationship. Was he even capable of that?

She knew he'd been married years ago, but his wife had passed unexpectedly. Since then, Robert had remained single. Maybe that death had made him wary of further relationships. Maybe if she reached out to him in that regard, by listing their commonalities, perhaps then he'd open up a little more.

But since their first meeting, he'd been distant. They'd randomly meet up for dinners when he came to town or he'd call once a month to check in, but she usually got the impression he was doing so because he felt he should and not because he actually wanted to.

"Everything all right?"

Ethan's question pulled her from her thoughts. Harper spun around and forced a smile.

"Fine. That was just my father."

No need to mention her father owned the resort. Ethan didn't strike her as the type looking for money, but it was still best to keep some things to herself for now. Besides, it wasn't like she was some kind of heiress. She wasn't expecting anything from Robert—except for the chance to build some kind of emotional connection.

Another chime sounded through the room, and this time Ethan pulled his cell from his pocket. He glanced at the screen, sighed, then shook his head.

"I need to deal with this," he told her. "Come to my room tonight."

That potent stare from several feet away was no less powerful than when he touched her bare skin with those big, strong hands. He always made her feel delicate…something she'd never felt before in her life.

"You already ordered me to be there," she reminded him, pretending like he didn't affect her. "If I'm free, I will come, but not because you say so."

Ethan chuckled as he started closing the distance between them. "You'll be there."

He stepped into her, laid his lips across hers and just as quickly stepped back.

"See you at seven."

"You said eight earlier," she reminded him.

He shot her a smile. "I want you sooner."

With a cocky whistle, Ethan turned and walked from the room, leaving her standing there irritated and completely turned on. Not that she'd ever let him know how much he affected her. Of course, someone as confident as Ethan probably already knew.

Well, she'd show him. She may be having his baby, but that didn't mean she had to jump at every command. She didn't know any other woman he'd had dealings with in the past, but Harper prided herself on being independent and unique.

Ethan Michaels might have finally met his match.

Four

"I guess he's held up in Barcelona," Ethan said, swirling the ice sphere in his bourbon. "The longer I wait, the more pissed off I get."

Granted, his edginess could have something to do with the fact he was still reeling from the bomb of impending fatherhood—and from the way that seven o'clock had come and gone over an hour ago without Harper arriving in his room.

He wasn't going to chase her down, and he wasn't going to beg. He'd never begged for a woman in his life, and he sure as hell wasn't going to start now... even if she carried his child.

"You're sounding a little edgier than usual," Dane stated.

His twin's statement pulled Ethan back. He set the tumbler on the bar and flattened his hand on the counter. Ethan thrived on control, especially over his own damn life, but here he was watching it play out and all he could do was wait.

"I'm fine," he ground out.

"Trying to convince yourself?" Dane asked.

"I just want this to be over and for me to have my resort back," Ethan insisted. "That's all."

He wasn't ready to announce the pregnancy.

"As soon as you do, Stella and I want to get married," Dane moved on. "We don't feel it's right until all this is settled. Plus, it will give us another reason to celebrate."

Dane deserved the happiness. Hell, they both did. After nearly twenty years of planning, working their asses off to regain money and power after having it stolen, this reckoning was long overdue.

"You keeping out of trouble while you wait on your family reunion?" Dane asked.

"Nothing I can't handle."

Maybe a lie, but whatever.

"Do you even know her name?" Dane chuckled.

Oh, he knew her name. He'd moaned it enough times while he learned every inch of Harper's curvy body, and damn if he wasn't itching to touch her again. Hell, he was in trouble. Not just because of the pregnancy, but because he'd let himself get agitated by a woman. He'd let her under his skin just enough that he was getting cranky without her.

Sex muddled the mind. That had initially been the reason he'd used it. He'd wanted that foggy state to numb the pain; he'd wanted to disappear outside reality for a time.

But Ethan had never been in this type of situation, and he refused to lose control over his emotions or get swept up in some spiral of feelings.

"I'll take that as a no," Dane replied.

Ethan pulled himself from his thoughts and cleared his throat. "I'll keep you posted on Robert, but I'm expecting him very soon. Go ahead and make those wedding plans."

Just the words *wedding plans* sent a shiver of terror through Ethan. He supposed some people went for that type of lifestyle, but he was just fine without a binding piece of paper, thank you very much.

"Oh, Stella is all set as soon as I give her the go-ahead," Dane laughed.

Ethan couldn't recall the last time he'd heard his brother laugh. The foreign sound actually had Ethan smiling himself. They'd waited so long to claim their own happiness, their destiny.

The chime from the private elevator echoed through the open penthouse. There was only one visitor he was expecting, and she was overdue.

"I'll keep you posted," Ethan promised. "Give Stella my love."

He ended the call and slid the cell back into his pocket, trying to pretend he wasn't anxious to see Harper step through that sliding door.

She'd kept him waiting, likely out of spite. For reasons he couldn't explain, he found that sexy as hell.

Ethan remained by the bar, resting his elbow on it and forcing himself not to react when she came in.

Moments later, the elevator whooshed open, and there she was. All sexy in a little floral skirt that wrapped around her hips, paired with a bright blue tank. The simple yet skimpy outfit showcased those lush curves even better than the dress she'd had on earlier, and while he might not know her well, he knew she'd changed on purpose. The little minx.

She stared at him across the penthouse, silence filling the space. Finally, she broke eye contact and started across the room like she belonged here.

"Dinner is cold," he told her as she passed by the domed plates on the dining table.

Harper ignored the table and moved into the living area, where she took a seat on the white sofa. She sank down and propped her long, dark legs up on the glass table. Her red-polished toes brushed the edge of the floral arrangement that the cleaning staff frequently changed out.

"I already ate," she stated, crossing her ankles and meeting his gaze. "I hope you didn't wait. I got held up."

Likely waiting him out just to prove she could.

"I didn't wait," he lied.

He hadn't eaten a bite. He'd been frustrated by her absence, worried over the pregnancy news, irritated at Robert for being so damn late. Too many emotions and not enough space in his head to store them all had soured his appetite.

"I wasn't late on purpose." She flashed him a grin as if she could read his mind, which only furthered his irritation. "I ran into a couple who couldn't find their restaurant, so I escorted them. Then when I left there, I ran into a little issue with a bellhop who was a little less than friendly, so I tried to smooth that over with the guests."

Ethan wouldn't put up with anything less than a loyal employee who respected each visitor that passed through their doors. He would make sure to keep an eye out and ears open for that subpar bellhop. He'd already been making mental notes of stellar employees he'd encountered. And the less-than-stellar ones.

"What made you intervene?" Ethan asked, taking his tumbler and crossing to the living area.

He rested his hip against the sofa across from where Harper sat. She stared up at him and shrugged.

"I think everyone should be treated with respect, and I figured the employee might be having a bad day. I was just trying to help."

Interesting.

"And did everything get worked out?" he asked.

A wide smile spread across her face. "Of course."

"So you design and you play referee." Ethan took a sip of his bourbon. "What other secrets do you keep?"

Harper laid a hand over her belly, and Ethan swallowed. No surprise there, but everything else about this woman was a mystery. He didn't know her, not in the ways a man should know a woman who was going to have his child.

"I think a few secrets are necessary, don't you?" she asked.

Considering he kept quiet about his true reason for being there, he would have to agree. But still, he didn't like not being in the know about everything that affected him. Shouldn't he know everything about the woman who was going to have his baby?

"I think there's more to you than what you show," he replied.

"That's a coping mechanism." She dropped her feet to the floor and crossed her legs, the move easing up the slit in her skirt. "Care to tell me what keeps your secrets bottled up?"

"Coping mechanism is a valid reason."

She'd completely nailed his reasoning for keeping his cards close to his chest. The little tidbits he uncovered kept revealing how their lives paralleled.

But right now, he wanted to intersect. Those legs all on display were tempting him to the point he was ready to unwrap that skirt and show her just how much he craved her.

"You've got that look in your eye," she murmured.

He gripped the tumbler. "And what look is that?"

Ignoring his question, Harper came to her feet, propped her hands on her hips and stared back without making a move toward him.

"You invited me here for sex," she said, crossing her arms and doing amazing things to her breasts in the process. "Dinner is a given."

"Well, you're here."

The corner of her mouth twitched, and he knew she wanted to smile. He had her. She couldn't dodge his advance, and she wasn't even trying. That wasn't vanity talking—it was the truth. And in all fairness, he was just as drawn to her...not that he'd admit any such thing.

"I'm here to discuss our child," she retorted. "We do have an obligation to make some sort of plan and keep our clothes on during the process."

"I'm well aware of what we need to do. When are you seeing a doctor?"

"Tomorrow," she told him. "Everything is set for this initial checkup. I'll have a few tests and an ultrasound, too."

Ethan started to close the distance between them. "Is there a problem?"

"Relax." Harper held up her hands and shook

her head. "Routine testing. It's all perfectly normal during a pregnancy."

"How do you know so much already?" he asked.

Harper laughed, and he hated how he suddenly felt like an ill-prepared moron. How was he not on top of this and more in control? He'd have to do some research and read up on pregnancies and babies. He had a feeling he was about to get an education he'd never planned on in his life.

"For one thing, I'm a woman, and I've had pregnant friends," she started. "We like to discuss such things over fancy dinners. Another thing, when I called my doctor, the nurse went over month by month what to expect during the appointments. I took some notes, but I also remember what she said. There's a lot that they test for, just as a matter of routine—checking the boxes to make sure there are no surprises."

Routine. Okay, he could handle that.

What the hell would he do if something went wrong? He knew absolutely nothing about babies or pregnancies. When he got together with his friends, it was to discuss his nightclubs or a limited-edition bottle of bourbon they'd purchased. On occasion they'd discuss trading in their jet or their car for the next upgrade. But never, not once, had the topic of children come up.

"I want to be with you during the doctor's visit."

Harper stared at him for a moment, and he

thought she was going to argue, but ultimately she nodded.

"I assumed as much," she said. "I wouldn't keep you out. No matter how all of this happened or how shocked we are, we're in this together if that's what you want."

"I want to be in my child's life." A ball of emotions rolled through him. "My mother passed when I was a teen, and I never knew my real father. There's no way I'd abandon you or this baby."

A soft smile spread across her face. She tipped her head, and he couldn't identify the look in her eyes.

"What?"

She took one step forward, then another. "You haven't shared much about your life. Just hearing you open up without me asking…it just means so much now."

There was no way to go through this with her and not get personal. As much as he kept his heart guarded, his life to himself, he couldn't be completely closed off to Harper. But he would have to decide how much to share and when to do so.

Once the resort reverted back to him, he wouldn't mind telling her everything. Right now, though, he just needed to focus on Robert.

But he still wanted to get to know more about Harper—especially when it came to her connection to his resort.

"Did you get any more planning done today?" he asked. "When we parted, you were talking about the ballroom."

"I called in my team, and we're going to get started." She positively beamed when she spoke. Obviously decorating was her passion. "The ballroom won't be where we begin, though. I'd like to start with the lobby, because I want the first major impact to be the focal point of the resort. I want guests to believe they've stepped into another world when they arrive."

Could she be more perfect?

For the job and to be the mother of his child. Not for him. But the vision he'd gotten a glimpse of was exactly how he wanted to renovate his mother's dream. All of this was falling into place so perfectly. Robert would foot the bill for a grand redesign just in time for Ethan to take over.

Oh, the victory was going to be sweet.

"And what are your thoughts for the lobby?" he asked, crossing to take a seat next to her on the sofa.

She stared at how close he sat, hip to hip, but not reaching for her in any other way. Yeah, he was just as surprised by his restraint, but the talk of the resort trumped his desires...for now.

Harper's eyes darted back to his face. "You want to talk about my work?"

Ethan stretched his arm along the couch behind her and nodded. "Yeah, I do."

He didn't need to justify his reasons. She'd already mentioned she wanted to get to know more about him, and turnabout was fair play. Besides, he'd rather start with her...with Mirage.

Harper's dark eyes narrowed before she shook her head and eased back into the cushions. "I was thinking of a water wall, something tranquil and serene. I want the guests to immediately relax, and water is proven to do that. Decorating isn't just about what looks pretty—it's about making people feel good about an experience."

Ethan listened to her, watched how she spoke with those delicate hands. Her eyes shone in a way he hadn't noticed before. The more she discussed the style, the more he knew his mother would have loved everything this resort would become.

And that was ultimately what he wanted. Of course he deserved to have this place back in his name, but once he was in charge, he had every intention of paying tribute to the remarkable woman who'd started it all.

He remembered her favorite color being green. Somewhere, in some place, he had to incorporate that shade. Perhaps in the Caribbean-themed restaurant or the Italian one. Something classy with green and white, maybe a touch of gold.

"You've put quite a lot of thought into this," he told her when she stopped talking and he'd logged his thoughts for later. "You ran through nearly every detail and didn't once look at a note in your phone."

Harper's mouth spread into a wide smile—the action sent a sucker punch right to his gut. How the hell did a grin have his breath catching in his throat? She'd flashed a saucy smile at him before, but nothing like this. She genuinely beamed.

"Because I have a vision and it's all in my head," she explained. "Every aspect of what I want to do with this place is like a living piece, and there's no way I'll forget a single one of them."

"But...you do have everything documented. Right?"

Harper rolled her eyes and laughed. "My sister would come back and haunt me if I didn't have everything documented and backed up."

"Did you work long with your sister before she passed?"

Damn it. He hadn't meant to ask. That was too personal, and a question that would only lead to exposing vulnerability.

"Not long enough," she murmured, her smile instantly fading. "I believe everything happens for a reason, but I just can't fathom why she was taken at such a young age. I mean, surely there was so much more for her to accomplish. You just don't realize how fragile life is until someone intimately close to you is gone. That sounds clichéd, but it's true."

Ethan had experienced those very same thoughts

for so long after his mother passed. He knew that pain, knew that aching void that nothing or no one could ever fill.

Ultimately, that's how he ended up living a reckless life, stumbling into owning and operating a string of profitable nightclubs and making billions. Yeah, everything happened for a reason, but he'd give it all back to have his mother.

"Then accomplish it for her," he finally stated.

Harper chewed her bottom lip for just a moment. Some women did that as a coy way to flirt, but he knew her well enough to know she wasn't playing some cutesy little game. Her thoughts were on her sister, on their business. Her loyalty and commitment were admirable traits, and as much as this whole baby news was still a shock, Harper had qualities he'd want his child to possess.

"I plan on doing just that," she confirmed. "Every job I take will be done in her honor. I won't fail, because I refuse to even allow the thought to enter my mind."

"Spoken like a true businesswoman."

Harper laughed and came to her feet. "I don't know about that. I never had my heart set on business, but I am creative and enjoy using my mind for work. I sort of just stumbled into the business part."

"That's how the best companies get started," he explained. "I never thought about going into business, either. Yet here I am."

Harper tipped her head to the side as her dark brows drew in. "And what are you, exactly? Jet-setting playboy tycoon?"

Ouch. That wasn't what he'd expected her to say. Clearly he hadn't made the best impression. Even though her description was dead on, he still didn't like the words coming out of her mouth.

Now he had to show the mother of his child—and prove to himself—that he was so much more. Because he was, damn it.

It was time for him to step up his game…and maybe open up that bank of emotions he'd kept on lockdown for nearly two decades.

Five

Maybe she shouldn't have thrown out such a label. From the pained expression on his face, she wasn't sure if he was reeling from the insult or trying to figure a way to defend himself.

"Ethan, I—"

"No." He held up a hand. "I'd say you're accurate. I work hard, I play hard. I won't apologize for the man I am. But at the same time, I'm not heartless and I'm not a bastard. I enjoy all aspects of my life, and sometimes I use coping mechanisms."

Sex. He used sex to cope…but what pain was he masking? Who had hurt him?

"Back to business," he said, circling around. "Because that's something where we can relate. I stumbled into my area as well, but after ten years, I'm damn good at what I do, and I couldn't imagine anything else."

"Nice dodge on your personal issues," she half joked.

With a mock nod, he smiled, and that gleaming grin had her nerves curling low in her belly. She had to remember even though he used sex as a line of defense, he still used it. She couldn't fall for his charms simply because he was irresistible and she carried his baby.

She'd done her fair share of using when it came to this fling…which was all the more reason to keep mentally reminding herself what this was and what it wasn't.

"So what is it that you do?" she prodded when he said nothing.

"I own nightclubs on both the East and the West Coasts. I'm acquiring a bistro in France, and I've been sniffing around a couple of pubs in Scotland. I plan to branch out globally and make a big impact."

Harper tried to hide her surprise. "Impressive résumé. I wouldn't have thought international business."

"Is this a job interview?" he asked with a quirk of his brow and a naughty grin.

"It wasn't, but since you're the father of my child, maybe we should dig deeper."

His smile slowly faded as the muscle in his jaw clenched. "My mother passed when I was a teenager, my stepfather was a bastard and stole my inheritance, and my twin brother is engaged. Oh, after the military I landed in a nightclub, got completely drunk for reasons that don't matter, and somehow that actually *did* turn into a job interview, which ultimately gave me my start as a business owner. And that brings us up to date."

Harper listened to the very abbreviated version of Ethan's life and figured he'd hit every highlight of what had caused him pain. But she opted to home in on the one area she hoped wasn't so crushing.

"You have a twin?"

Something in his dark features softened. "Dane. He lives in Montana on a ranch."

Harper laughed. "Quite the opposite of your beach-bum life."

"Quite the opposite of me," Ethan muttered in agreement. "He's kept to himself since Mom died, so the fact that he met someone who could penetrate that wall… She must be amazing."

"You don't know her?"

Ethan shook his head and came back to his feet. "We haven't met. Dane and I have been working on a project for a while that has kept us apart. We email or talk on the phone, but I haven't seen him for a few years."

There it was again. That pain.

Ethan paced to the wall of windows and stared out at the moonlight shining down onto the ocean. Harper knew she couldn't let this moment pass.

"You know, my sister has only been gone six months, and that void is unlike anything I've ever known."

Harper rose but didn't cross to him. She just felt like she should be on level field or be ready…for whatever.

"I don't know how I'll feel once years pass," she went on. "The thought of not seeing her is something I still can't fathom."

Ethan glanced over her shoulder. "It's not that I don't want to see him. I love my brother. But something shifted when our mom died. We dealt with the loss so differently. Then we were so set on trying to care for ourselves after our stepdad left us with nothing."

He turned back to the window, his shoulders rigid, his hands shoved in his pockets. Harper's eyes darted around the space, and she spotted the half-empty tumbler on the bar in the corner.

"Dane and I went into the army," he went on, his tone calm, yet broken. "We kept in contact, but it was so random and the interactions were spaced farther and farther apart. Then we banded together and decided to go after the bastard who stole from us."

Intrigued, Harper took one step, then another. Before she realized, she stood right behind him.

"Did you catch him?" she asked. "I hope you left him penniless and suffering. Stealing from kids after the loss of their mother is a new level of asshole."

With a mock laugh, Ethan turned to face her. "Oh, he's in his own league. But no. We haven't caught up with him yet. Soon. Very soon."

Harper knew Ethan would stop at nothing to seek revenge, and she honestly couldn't say she blamed him. He'd had years to let this anger fester and build.

"So is that what brings you here?" she asked, reaching up to smooth the frown lines between his brows.

Ethan gripped her wrist and pulled her arm behind her back, making her arch against him. "I'm done talking about him. There's only one person I want to focus on right now."

Harper's body responded—the tingling from head to toe had her closing her eyes and waiting on those lips to cover hers. Despite having told him no more sex, Harper wasn't sure she was strong enough to turn him away.

She was here, wasn't she?

But a moment later, Ethan released her, and she stumbled to keep herself upright. Harper opened her eyes and glanced around to see Ethan striding toward the kitchen. He removed dome lids from the plates on the long island. She hadn't even noticed the dishes there before.

"Sit down," he demanded. "You need to eat."

Harper remained in place, crossing her arms over her chest. "I ate dinner."

"Well, you're eating for two now."

She didn't even try to prevent the eye roll. "I always thought that saying was so silly. A tiny fetus doesn't need a large meal."

Ethan stared at her a moment before shrugging. "I don't know a damn thing about pregnancies, but I read that pregnant women might need frequent meals, and I thought you should eat."

Harper stared at the spread and realized he'd ordered all this food…for her. Well, for the baby, but the fact he truly cared and wasn't completely about ripping her clothes off was a little sweet.

But only a little. She couldn't blow his gestures out of proportion. That would mean she wanted him to be kind and do cutesy things.

Ugh. Her hormones were all over the place.

"I don't know what to do here," he admitted. "But if you could come eat some fruit or something. Hell, whatever."

Well, wasn't that adorable? Someone was insecure and fumbling over his words. Yet seconds ago he'd been more than in control when he'd had her arched against him and silently begging him for more.

The man likely wasn't used to being anything but in total control. Considering their current situation of being thrust into parenthood, she'd say that control would be a long time coming for both of them.

"Did you eat?" she asked, making her way to the wooden bar stool.

He nodded and pulled out a bottle of water from the fridge and set it in front of her.

"So you intend for all of this to be for me?" Harper laughed and selected a plump raspberry. "Have you ever seen me eat this much?"

She popped the piece of fruit into her mouth and welcomed the delicious burst of flavor. Maybe she was a little hungry, but she'd never admit as much.

"I wanted to make sure you had a good variety," he defended.

"There's enough variety here for the entire third floor."

Ethan's lips curved into another toe-curling grin. "I'll take that as a thanks for my gesture."

Harper grabbed a handful of blueberries. "And is that why you did this? So I'd be indebted to you and reward you as you see fit?"

"Talking dirty to me will get you everywhere."

"Do you think of anything besides sex?"

Ethan's intense stare stretched across the island, making her wish she could take those words back.

"My mind is typically on work," he finally answered. "But when I'm around you, those thoughts become a little muddled."

"Should I be flattered?"

Ethan circled the island and took a blueberry from her hand and held it up to her lips. "Flattered isn't what I want you to feel."

Her gaze dropped to that mouth that had caused her so much pleasure. When she shifted her focus back to his eyes, there was that passion, that desire she'd come to recognize from him.

"So we are back to sex," she murmured, taking the berry from between his fingertips. She might have bitten him lightly, but just so he knew who was in charge here.

"Even though you're carrying my child…" He stopped, shook his head and blew out a sigh. "*Especially* because you're carrying my child, I want you more than ever. Maybe we should cool it, maybe we should end this fling, but I keep asking myself why. We're adults who more than enjoy each other's company, and we both have outside issues that are put aside when we're together."

She'd been telling herself those same things. Granted, she'd also told herself she needed to keep her clothes on around Ethan from here on out, but suddenly everything he said made sense. Why shouldn't she seek this happiness, even if for only a few moments longer? There was no rule that just because he wasn't putting a ring on her finger, they couldn't continue their passionate nights until it was time for one of them to leave.

Right?

He took another blueberry and slid it back and forth across her lips. When she opened, he pulled the fruit away and covered her lips with his.

Harper fisted her hands in her lap to prevent herself from reaching for him. A woman had to maintain some sort of self-control. But the way he made love to her mouth only had her wondering if that was a promise of more to come. The man made a kiss a full-body assault, because there wasn't a spot on her that wasn't ready for more of his touch.

Ethan eased back; that smirk on his face and gleam in his eye had her gritting her teeth. He wanted her to beg, but she had more pride than that. This was still a fling, and she could walk away at any moment.

Without a word, he popped the berry into his mouth as he trailed his fingers up her bare arms. Oh, damn. She should've walked away before now. But she'd known what would happen when she came here. She was a glutton—there was no denying the fact she still wanted him. It wasn't smart, but she was human and had wants and needs she wouldn't deny herself.

Maybe one more time. She'd let this happen once more and then they'd start discussing the future and their child.

"You're thinking too hard," he murmured against her ear. "You're mentally arguing with yourself about being here."

"I couldn't stay away."

The truth slid from her lips before she could stop herself. It was almost like the man had cast some magical spell over her. She knew it was happening, and she simply didn't care.

"You made me wait," he scolded. "You did that on purpose."

"Maybe," she admitted.

His lips grazed the side of her neck, and Harper dropped her head to the side to allow him all the access he needed.

"I never thought a headstrong woman would appeal to me."

Huh? Did that mean he was attracted to her for more than a heated fling? No, that's not what he meant. It couldn't be.

For a split second, Harper thought about calling him on his statement, but those clever lips eased down to the scoop in her tank and the next thing she knew his hands were working the knot on her skirt.

Yes. This was what she ached for, what she needed. Just once more, right?

Ethan's hands seem to be all over her, and she couldn't escape the moan as he yanked the knot on her skirt and the material fell to either side of her hips. Ethan wasted no time in pulling her panties down her legs as his mouth worked over her breasts through the thin material of her tank top.

Harper reached for the hem and slid the shirt over her head and off to the side as she kicked away the panties around her ankles. Ethan's eyes devoured her the second he reached around and expertly flicked her bra open. In no time, that unwanted garment had been tossed carelessly away, as well.

Strong hands encircled her waist and lifted her onto the cold island. Harper let out a squeal of surprise but heated all over again when Ethan came to stand between her parted legs.

"You want me to stop?" he asked, his eyes holding hers.

"No," she whispered.

A flare of hunger flashed through his eyes before he dropped to his knees and gripped her inner thighs. Harper bit the inside of her cheek to keep from begging or crying out before he'd even done anything other than drive her mad from want.

She threaded her fingers through his hair as he dropped light kisses from her knee to the point where she ached most. Then he moved to the other leg, and Harper gripped harder.

With a chuckle, Ethan finally settled right where she wanted him. He held onto her hips and jerked her closer to the edge of the counter as he made love to her.

Bursts of euphoria spiraled through her. He'd never done this—nobody had ever done this. She'd never let anyone get that intimate with her. Insecurities and all that.

But Ethan wasn't just anybody.

There was no way to describe all of the delicious tingles coursing through her from his hands, his mouth. She didn't want this moment to end, didn't want to lose this perfect moment of euphoria.

After several minutes of the most exquisite pleasure, her entire body tightened as the experience became too much. Her fingers tightened in his hair, and there was no holding back the cries of pleasure.

Ethan nipped at her inner thigh when her trembling ceased.

"Harper?"

His husky tone broke through her haze, and she realized her eyes were squeezed shut. Coming back down from her high, Harper focused her attention on the man who now stood before her wearing a smile.

"You good?" he asked.

Good? That was such a mild, calm word for the storm that had just wrecked her in the most perfect, amazing way.

"I'll take speechlessness as a positive sign." He leaned forward and nipped at her earlobe. "Now, finish eating, since I distracted you."

Wait…what? Eat? He could think about food at a time like this?

Ethan turned and rounded the counter. Harper glanced over her shoulder, more than aware that one of them was totally naked while the other was fully dressed and picking out a cube of cheese.

"Are you serious?" she asked, easing down off the counter and rounding up her clothes.

He popped a piece of gouda into his mouth and stared across the space. "About food? Yeah. You barely ate."

Harper slid into her panties, then her skirt. Clutching her bra and tank, she pulled in a shaky breath.

"Are you playing a game?"

Ethan's brows narrowed. "Game?"

Harper didn't know if she was more confused or irritated. "Are we not going to finish what we started?"

"By my recollection, you finished—enthusiastically."

Yeah. Definitely irritated. She pulled on her bra and tank, needing the extra armor.

"You didn't."

Ethan shrugged. "I'll live. Are you complaining?"

No, that would make her a bitch.

"I've never met a man like you," she muttered.

Ethan let out a bark of laughter. "I'll take that as a compliment."

She continued to stare as he grabbed a small plate and started adding a variety of fruits and cheese, plus a small finger sandwich. Then he set it in front of the stool she'd been on before he blew her mind.

"Take a seat," he told her. "You can eat and tell me more about your renovation ideas."

She wasn't sure what his angle was by playing her and keeping her guessing, but she wasn't about to let her guard down. She was going to figure out Ethan Michaels one way or another...something she should've done before he permanently landed in her life.

Six

The next morning Ethan was still questioning who the hell he'd become. Since when did he have a willing woman—a sexy-as-hell willing woman—naked and ready for him, and not take full advantage of the situation?

With the time difference between California and France, Ethan had finally gotten out of bed at 4:00 a.m. after a restless night. He'd made yet another call to his Realtor to see where they stood on the final bid they'd put in on the waterfront bistro.

And yet it wasn't his latest quest that had his mind occupied or his sleep lacking. He knew he'd get the property, but he didn't know what the hell he was going to do with Harper.

She'd been naked, panting, sitting atop the island in his kitchen. He'd given her an orgasm and what did he do next? Not take her to the bedroom or even take her right there on the floor.

No, he'd made her a charcuterie board and they'd chatted until midnight about water walls, open courtyards with lush plants, infinity pools and special couples' rooms for secret fetishes.

She'd thought of every aspect of this adults-only resort, and maybe that's what had him so distracted. He'd come here for the sole purpose of gaining back what should have been his. Hearing Harper talk about the future makeovers had him itching to get Mirage in his name sooner than ever.

So now he was sexually frustrated, confused at his own actions and not so patiently waiting to hear about his bid.

Ethan padded to his kitchen to make coffee, but his eyes landed on the island. As if he needed the reminder of how damn sexy she'd been, utterly bare, completely at his mercy and more than willing to give him more.

But something shifted after hearing her speak of her late sister and seeing the way Harper was so determined to complete her job despite having been dealt the bombshell of a pregnancy. The level of admiration he had for her now was something he hadn't expected, and he needed to sort it out before he made a fool of himself and she mistook his generosity for something more.

There could be no *more*. He was too busy, too devoted to his businesses. Not only had he had a mentor who had entrusted him with the nightclubs, but Ethan had branched out on his own. He'd made something of himself when everything had been stripped away. There was no way in hell he'd let anything or anyone sever the strings he'd so delicately forged to keep his life stable.

Not to mention the fact he and his twin were attempting to rebuild their relationship that had been upset when their mother passed. They'd each dealt with the loss in their own ways…opposite ways. Those ultimately pulled them in different directions.

So, no. Ethan didn't have the room in his life to add in more. While he would never, ever turn away his child and he fully intended on being a hands-on dad, he wasn't about to entertain the idea of a relationship with Harper.

Thankfully, she had her own agendas and felt the same about long-term commitments. They'd have to come to some common ground for co-parenting. He wouldn't give up any of his career, and he would never ask her to, either. They could work together to make everything work in the best interest of the three of them.

Ignoring the island as much as he could, Ethan brewed a cup of coffee and headed out onto his private balcony overlooking the Pacific Ocean. The view never grew old. Ever. Perhaps that's why he had been so willing to take over the nightclubs that were on the coasts. He needed that view, that freedom that came with staring out at the expanse of water and dreaming of bigger, better things. There was always another conquest to obtain, always another goal to reach.

He waited until he was halfway through his cup of coffee before he gave in and texted Harper. Last night they'd discussed breakfast but hadn't made any definite plans. He also knew she was a morning person, and the sun was up, so he figured so was she.

My place. Breakfast.

Ethan set his phone on the side table next to his patio chair and sipped his coffee. A second later the vibration caught his attention. He gave the screen a glance and smiled.

Already ordered room service. Should be there any minute.

And a second later, the chime on his intercom alerted him to a guest wanting to come up to his penthouse.

He'd never thought a take-charge woman would be attractive, mostly because he thrived on calling any and all shots. But something about Harper and her assertiveness turned him the hell on.

Within five minutes, his concierge had delivered quite the spread and had set it all up on the balcony. Ethan started to tip, but the young man said it had already been taken care of by Miss Williams.

He wasn't sure he'd ever had a woman a step ahead of him. Ethan wasn't quite sure what to make of that, but one thing was certain. He liked it.

Damn that woman for making him want her more than he ever should.

The elevator chimed once again, indicating a visitor. She had the pass code, so he didn't have to ring her up anymore.

The door slid open, and Harper stepped out. Her hair had been piled up on her head, stray curls tumbling down around her neck. She sported some red bathing suit cover-up with that damn red bikini beneath.

It was those tiny red scraps of material that had drawn him in to begin with. Was she purposely taunting him? Not that he needed any help in finding her desirable.

"I'd kill for a cup of coffee," she stated, marching through his penthouse and straight to the balcony.

He followed her out. "I'll make you a cup."

"No," she growled, shaking her head. "I'm trying to really be good because of the baby."

"You can't have coffee?" he asked, holding on to his own mug.

"Too much caffeine isn't good." She grabbed

the pitcher of orange juice and poured a hearty glass. "I mean, I could have one cup, but I'd rather not."

He probably should figure out all the dos and don'ts regarding pregnancy.

"Are you feeling okay?" he asked, setting his mug down on the table and getting a glass of juice for himself.

"I'm starving and tired. And also a little nauseated, but I think I just need to eat."

She eyed his discarded mug. "You know, you can still drink that. I'm not offended."

With a shrug, Ethan reached for a plate. "I didn't think you were offended, but I don't see any reason why I can't do this journey with you."

She stared another minute before shaking her head and muttering something he couldn't quite make out.

They made their plates in silence and settled into the corner at the table for two beneath a bright yellow umbrella.

The moment they sat down, Harper made a face and held on to her stomach.

"Maybe eggs weren't a good idea," she mumbled.

Ethan stilled. "Are you going to be sick?"

Harper closed her eyes and seemed to be taking some deep breaths. Without waiting for an answer, he took her plate away. If the eggs were the culprit, he'd throw them all out.

He took the plate and the dish of omelets into his kitchen.

When he came back out, Harper wasn't looking so ill.

"Sorry about that," she stated, glancing up to him when he approached the table. "I read that smells can affect you more strongly when you're pregnant, but I hadn't experienced that yet. So, eggs are definitely out. Well, unless they're in a cake. Then I'm sure they're fine."

Ethan laughed, thankful she was feeling better and still had her sense of humor.

His cell vibrated in the pocket of his shorts just as he sat. He spared her a glance as he pulled the phone out.

"Excuse me," he stated before glancing to the screen.

His investigator. Not a call he wanted to put off, since his investigator wasn't one to call just to chat. There had to be a development where Robert was concerned.

"I need to take this," he told Harper.

"Oh, go ahead." She waved a hand in his direction. "I'm fine."

Another reason to be attracted to her. She didn't demand his undivided attention, and she understood the importance of work.

Ethan moved to the other side of the balcony and answered the call.

"Marcus. What's up?"

"Nothing dire, but something I found interesting in Robert's communication with his assistant."

Ethan gripped the phone as he stared out onto the calm ocean. "What was said?"

"Apparently Robert is making his way there, which you know, and he should be landing in the next day or so."

"And?" Ethan prompted.

"We know he has a daughter based on his background checks, but he's never mentioned her publicly. This is the first time since we've been tracking recently that he's actually going to see her in person. Apparently, she's staying at Mirage."

"She's here?" Ethan asked.

He didn't know anything about Robert's daughter except that she existed. He had no intention of involving an innocent in his quest for revenge. Everything going on was between him, Dane and their stepfather.

"I figure since you're there, maybe you could look her up."

"Give me her name."

It would be useful to at least know who she was so he could keep an eye on her for when her father showed. The old bastard might try to sneak in and out.

"Harper Williams."

Ethan stilled, his gaze jerking across the balcony to the woman in question.

"She's going to have dark curly hair, dark eyes. Her mother is Jamaican, and you know the father."

"I know exactly what she looks like," Ethan muttered.

Ethan disconnected the call without another word. Keeping an eye on Robert Anderson's daughter would be no problem at all…considering she was the mother of his child.

Seven

Harper smoothed a hand over her belly, which wasn't flat and never had been. But she couldn't wait to feel the baby bump, the little kicks—she'd even heard women discuss baby hiccups.

Despite being dealt the blow of a child when she wasn't even in a committed relationship, she wasn't sorry she was going to be a mother. Sure, the timing wasn't the best, but she couldn't help but wonder how Carmen would've reacted to the news of being an aunt.

Having a baby was exciting…this morning queasiness, not so much.

Ethan came back to the table, and she prayed her berries and croissant stayed down. She'd been feeling a little saucy this morning when she donned her bikini, but yacking all over the place would surely ruin her sassy vibe. Just when she was sort of getting the hang of this newfound confidence...

Every thought vanished when she saw Ethan's face.

"Everything okay?" she asked.

He hesitated a moment before grabbing his cloth napkin and placing it in his lap. With a forced smile, he nodded.

"Just some interesting developments with work. Nothing I can't handle."

"It's awfully early for work to already be catching you off guard."

"Time means nothing in my line of work," he informed her. "With things running on two coasts, plus my acquisition in France, I work all hours."

Harper smiled. "Then maybe you better get that coffee back, because you look like you need something stronger than juice."

His eyes raked over her, and she couldn't help but tremble.

"I'm sure it's nothing a sexy woman in a red bikini couldn't cure."

A wave of dizziness hit her that had nothing to do with his charming words. Harper closed her eyes and pulled in a slow breath, willing the moment to pass.

"Harper?"

His firm yet gentle grip on her arm had her shaking her head slightly.

"Give me just a minute."

He didn't say another word, but she heard his chair scrape against the concrete floor and the next instant she was swept up into his strong arms. Harper didn't protest as she laid her head on his shoulder, but she kept her eyes closed. The nausea seemed to be subsiding, but she wasn't so independent that she'd turn down the most romantic gesture known to woman.

When he laid her down, Harper lifted her lids and focused on his face, which was so, so close to hers.

"Okay?" he asked, obviously worried.

"It comes and goes," she stated, settling into the sofa cushions. "No need to worry. The doctor said this was normal. It's just annoying."

"You looking like you're ready to pass out isn't normal to me."

Aww. He cared. His instant reaction wasn't an act. She wasn't used to someone other than her sister showing concern for her, and as independent she was, there was no way she could deny that having someone care made her feel special.

"I assure you, I'm fine." She patted the side of his face. "But this is adorable."

Ethan's lips thinned, his brows drawing in as he eased back and stared down at her. "I'm not adorable," he grumbled.

Harper closed her eyes and rested her arm across her forehead. "Well, I think so. I'm feeling better, by the way. The dizzy spells just started yesterday, and they don't last long."

"I think you should stay here."

Harper lifted her arm slightly and opened one eye. "I'm here, aren't I?"

"You should stay in my suite for as long as we're both at the resort," he amended. "It's ridiculous for us both to have a place, and mine is larger."

Harper listened to what he said but didn't say a word.

"With a better view," he added.

"I'm not just playing house with you while we're here." Harper let out a mock laugh. "You're not serious."

"Do I look like I'm joking?"

Ethan eased down to sit on the table in front of the sofa.

Harper shifted to look at him as his idea ran over and over in her mind. Why on earth would he suggest such a thing? He didn't want a relationship any more than she did.

"Is this because I wasn't feeling well?" she asked. "Because that's certainly no reason for me to move my suitcases up here."

"You're having my child, and I want to make sure you and our baby are taken care of. That's not too much to ask, is it?"

Not when he phrased it like that, but still. Why did she need a keeper? She'd gotten along this far in life without someone hovering over her. She and Carmen always looked out for each other, but that was different.

She and Ethan were obviously still attracted to each other, the baby threw out the whole "fling" thing and now they had to make some tougher decisions.

They were adults who wanted the same things: freedom, career and a good time. There wouldn't be any messy complications, even if the whole pregnancy thing would eventually make things a little tricky. They were both on board with no relationships.

Sex, though…she'd be a fool to turn down twenty-four-hour access to that body.

"I'll think about staying here with you," she informed him, unable to hide her smile.

"Sounds like a yes to me."

Harper started to sit up, but he placed his hands on her shoulders.

"No rush," he said, easing her back down. "I can bring in your breakfast."

"I think I'm done with food for the time being."

She settled deeper into the cushions and stared up at the white beams stretching across the ceiling. Her designer eye loved how the penthouse seemed to be its own private beach house. The cozy style of the beams and the openness to the ocean breeze.

The wall of windows and balcony doors were elements she hoped to incorporate into more rooms. She definitely planned on upgrading all of the oceanfront suites to have more of an airy, relaxing feel.

"You're working."

Harper glanced to Ethan at his accusation. "Guilty."

"You had that look on your face," he said with a grin. "I know because I've seen it in the mirror."

"I just can't wait to dig in to this place. My team will be here next week, and I've spoken to the manager so we can hopefully have a nice, smooth transition from one area to the next and not disrupt the guests too much."

"Maybe adding in some perks would be the way to go," he suggested.

Now she did sit up—slowly, but she was feeling better.

"What do you mean?" she asked.

"Nobody wants to be inconvenienced at all when they plan a getaway," he explained. "Maybe for the duration of the renovations, couple's massages could be free with a one-time limit per stay. Or one free room service meal. Just something so they know you're aware of their needs. People save and spend quite a bit to come here."

Harper listened to him, taking in his suggestion and fully intending to run it by her father's assistant.

"I wouldn't think someone like you would ever have a thought about saving money now that you have everything you want," she finally stated.

Ethan's face tightened, the muscle in his jaw clenched. "There was a time in my life where I watched every single dollar that came in and out. Just because I have a padded account now doesn't mean I'm not aware of other people's perspectives."

Never in her wildest dreams would she have guessed jet-setting playboy Ethan Michaels cared so deeply about how others lived. But everything he suggested sounded so perfect, she only wished she had thought of the idea before.

"You're a pretty smart businessman," she joked.

"I refused to be anything but smart when it comes to business."

His tone left no room for humor, and Harper had to admire him even more. There were so many layers to Ethan, and part of her wished she was at a point in her life where she could look for a husband. Eventually she did want a family and a loving man, but she had to devote her life to Two Sisters and to her child for now.

Part of her couldn't help but wonder if this baby was a special gift. Like maybe she was being given another chance at family after her sister's passing.

She'd never given much thought to faith or the idea of a grand plan before, but with her mother off gallivanting who knows where, her father not much of a hands-on guy and her sister gone, maybe this was just a blessing in disguise.

"I think I'll have the concierge bring my things up later this afternoon," she finally said, circling back to the offer. "If you're sure you won't get sick of me."

Ethan's smile widened, the naughty gleam in his eye stirring her body.

"Oh, I'm sure. In fact, I think we should get married."

Eight

"Married?" Harper screeched.

Ethan had to admit the words that had come out of his mouth had surprised the hell out of him, too. But he wasn't about to retract them. This was Robert Anderson's biological daughter. No way in hell could he let this prime opportunity pass him by.

Obviously he never would've mentioned marriage had she not been pregnant, but why not?

"I know we both agreed that we're not the marrying type of people," he started as the idea blossomed inside his head. "And I'm not saying I'm ready for the whole ordeal of marriage, but think about this for a minute. We are both driven in our careers, so we get each other. We both want what's best for this child."

Harper blinked, then shook her head. Yeah, the idea was absurd, but the longer it was out in the open, the more he found himself wanting this to happen.

The reasons for his insane demand were mounting. His mother had been single, raising two boys on her own for quite some time before Robert had entered the picture. But his baby had a father who badly wanted to be part of its life. Given that, where was the logic in him living somewhere else and having to shuttle the kid back and forth between them? There was no way he'd want to give up any amount of custody of his own child. But the real reason he was pushing for marriage, if he were being completely honest, was that he wanted every single leg up on Robert Anderson he could get.

"That's it?" she asked. "Because we both like to work and we want a well-rounded kid, you think we should marry?"

Ethan shrugged, not backing down, but not about to beg. "People have been married for less."

"And divorced in no time when the marriage fails."

"I don't fail," he countered. "Ever."

Harper stared at him, but his gaze didn't waver. The more she pushed, the more he had to see this through. This was the riskiest, most asinine move he'd ever made, but the payoff would be everything.

Dane would have already called him a dumb ass and told him to think this through, but Ethan *had* thought it through...for a few seconds, anyway.

"I can't just marry you," she repeated.

"Think about it."

He came to his feet and started back toward the balcony. He could at least wheel the cart inside so he could finish his breakfast. Harper might pick around, too, if the food was in front of her.

"Think about it?" she mocked at his back. "You tell me to think about it and then walk away?"

He spared a glance over his shoulder. "I'm hungry."

By the time he had moved their breakfast and drinks back inside, Harper didn't look like she wanted to rip his head off anymore, but she still kept that questioning gaze locked on him.

"What changed?" she asked once he took a seat in the cushy white chair next to her. "You never wanted a relationship."

"I still don't," he explained. "This is nothing more than business. We both want what's best for our baby, and we're both workaholics. It's the perfect merger, really."

Harper stood and crossed to the cart, where she poured herself another glass of juice. "A merger."

"Are you going to keep repeating everything I say?"

She turned to face him with a smirk that made him wonder if he would get her to come around. He wouldn't have it any other way. Ethan never backed down from a challenge, and Harper, their baby and Robert Anderson were all part of his past, present and future. No challenge, no *payoff*, had ever been more important.

"Are you going to keep insisting this is a good idea?" she retorted.

Ethan crossed his ankle over his knee and leaned back in the chair. He didn't want to appear anxious or worried. He was neither of those. What he was, was determined, and that's precisely how he'd gotten this far.

"If you can move beyond the shock of my proposal—"

"Is that what that was?" she mocked, taking a seat back on the sofa and curling her legs to the side.

"Of sorts," he conceded.

Harper gripped her juice glass and stared down at the contents. Ethan waited, letting the kernel of an idea roll around in her head. She seemed skeptical, but she was still in discussion, so he wasn't discounting her just yet. He had a way of being persuasive.

"You can't just ask me to marry you as some sort of business plan," she argued, but her voice lacked the heat it once had. He was winning her over.

Dane had always said Ethan was the reckless

one, the twin who jumped headfirst into things without thinking them through.

Well, here he was again. Wait until Dane heard about all of this.

"I figured you'd appreciate an honest, laid-out plan," he stated. "We marry, we raise our child together, we don't have to get our attorneys involved. We both can continue doing what we love and have someone who understands and is actually supportive at our sides while we share the parenting responsibilities."

Harper pursed her lips and leveled a stare at him. "And what happens when you want another woman or I see a guy I'm interested in?"

Ethan didn't hesitate to leap from his chair, circle the table and brace himself over her. With one hand on the arm of the sofa and the other on the back near her shoulder, he leaned down so there was no question about how serious he was on this topic.

"There will be no other men," he growled. "My wife will be in my bed and only my bed. I won't share."

Most people would be intimidated by his snarl and low tone, but Harper continued to stare, and she even had the nerve to pat his jaw and smile.

"Calm down there, sweetheart. Your proposal is getting less and less attractive." She narrowed her dark eyes and flattened her palm on his cheek. "There had better not be any other women, either. I also don't share."

A burst of accomplishment spread through him.

"Is that a yes?" he asked, inching closer.

When she didn't say a word, Ethan shifted to slide one hand over her bare thigh. He watched as her lids lowered for the briefest of seconds, her breath caught on a sharp inhale. Without taking his eyes off her face, Ethan trailed his fingertips over her stomach, straight up to the little knot tied between her breasts.

"I… I never said yes," she muttered.

"But you're thinking about it."

He gave the tie an expert yank, allowing the scraps of material to fall aside.

Harper closed her eyes and chewed on her lip. He had her…in every way he wanted her. She'd marry him; she'd be in his bed. He'd ultimately have his revenge on her father. He worried how she'd react, but he had to keep moving with this plan and take baby steps when it came to Harper. He had to choose his words, his actions, carefully so she didn't completely hate him at the end. He had to make her understand his side once everything was out in the open.

There was no way Robert Anderson deserved a daughter like Harper, and the man sure as hell would have no part in the life of Ethan's child.

"I'm not thinking at all right now," she told him as he cupped her full breast in his palm.

Ethan eased his other hand behind her back, pulling her forward until she sprawled over his sofa. He wanted her on display before him. A body like Harper's was meant to be worshipped.

"Are you feeling better?" he asked, realizing he should've asked before now, but damn it, he couldn't resist her.

The health of her and the baby came above all else, though. Even his revenge against Robert would have to come second to Harper and the child.

"I'm feeling pretty good." Harper reached for him, her fingertips curling around his shoulders. "Don't stop, Ethan. And don't deny yourself like last night."

Oh, he fully planned on making sure they were both pleasured.

"You wore this on purpose," he accused, pulling her sheer cover-up off her shoulders. "Did you want to drive me crazy?"

Her delicate mouth tipped into a smile. "Maybe."

Ethan's body stirred at the little minx beneath him. That red material against her dark skin shouldn't be such a turn-on, but hell if it wasn't. Harper exuded sex and fantasies. Every time he had her, he wanted more. Now was no exception.

Harper wriggled out of the cover-up and the bikini top. He loved that a curvy woman had the confidence to wear something so sexy, so skimpy.

He hooked his thumbs in the waist of her little

bottoms and eased them down her silky legs and flung the garment over his shoulder.

"You better take off those shorts fast," she warned. "Because I was cheated last night."

Ethan pulled his shorts off and laughed. "You were more than satisfied, so I'm not sure how you were cheated."

Her fingers ran over his abs, and his arousal spiked.

"Because I didn't get to see or touch you," she told him. "Not like I wanted."

"Then by all means." Ethan settled onto the sofa and eased back into the corner of the sectional. "Have your way."

Harper came to her feet. She tucked stray tendrils behind her ears as her eyes raked over his bare body. There was such a hunger, one that matched his own, staring back at him.

When her focus shifted to his eyes, Harper took a step forward and lifted a knee. She settled her legs on either side of his hips, perfectly straddling his lap. Her breasts came right in front of his face and Ethan wasted no time in reaching for her with both hands.

"If I marry you, there will be rules." She rested her hands on either side of his head and leaned down. "My rules."

"Yes, ma'am."

His body ached for her to join them and right

now. He'd agree to anything she said. He'd never been at a woman's mercy before, but she was doing a damn good job of calling the shots now.

Harper leaned down and captured his lips beneath hers as she sank down onto him, finally joining their bodies.

She eased her hips back and forth, going much too slowly for his liking. Ethan took a firm grip of her hips, holding her in place while he set a new rhythm.

Harper let out a sharp cry, followed by a moan, so clearly she wasn't complaining. With her eyes shut, she tossed her head back and braced her palms on his chest. Her short nails bit into his skin, and he had to hold back his own groan at the delicious sting of pain.

Ethan held on to her hips, loving how she felt like a woman with all those luscious curves. They were so compatible, so in tune with each other.

Marrying her would be the best decision on both fronts.

Harper let out another cry of pleasure as her body tightened around his. She eased down onto his chest and claimed his lips once more as her climax hit her. He wasn't far behind.

Those lips of hers could make a man come undone all on their own. But it was her sweet little pants and cries that had him following her into oblivion.

Ethan fell into the moment and didn't worry about what would come next. She'd all but agreed to the marriage, and Ethan wanted this to happen fast. Before Robert arrived…and before he came to his senses.

Nine

"Say that again."

Ethan chuckled at his brother's response, but Dane wasn't joking. What the hell was his twin thinking?

"I said I'm getting married," Ethan repeated. "It's sudden, I know, but I promise you'll meet her."

"Are you out of your damn mind?" Dane growled, earning him a questioning stare from Stella across the room.

Dane gripped the cell and came to his feet, suddenly unable to sit still and listen to this nonsense.

"Who the hell is she?" Dane asked. "I just spoke to you a couple days ago, and you made no mention of any woman. Now suddenly you're getting married?"

Stella's eyes widened as he neared. Dane shrugged, because he couldn't make sense of this crazy notion of his brother's, either. Ethan had always been one to make rash decisions, but marriage at a time like this? What the hell? He'd never been serious about a woman, let alone mentioning he ever wanted that lifestyle.

"I'm marrying Robert's biological daughter."

Dane stilled. He reached for the back of the sofa and kept his gaze on his fiancée. She reached for his hand on the cushion and squeezed, offering him silent reassurance.

"Robert's daughter?" Dane repeated. "You're not seriously using a woman to get to—"

"No. I'm not a complete bastard," Ethan scoffed. "I had no idea who her father was when we started sleeping together. We were just a fling, and then she ended up pregnant and now I find out—"

"Pregnant?" Dane yelled.

Stella closed her eyes and shook her head. Yeah, that pretty much mimicked his internal reaction, as well.

"What the hell, man?"

"Obviously I didn't mean for that to happen," Ethan retorted. "Everything has snowballed here, and I'm doing the best with the situation I've been dealt."

"The best? You're calling this your best?" Dane slid his hand from beneath Stella's and reached up to rub his head, which suddenly started pounding. "You're bringing a child into this chaos? Are you even thinking of the goal we agreed on?"

"You think I'm not set out to take Robert down?" Ethan demanded. "That's all I've wanted since Mom died. We're so close, I'm not letting anything get in the way."

Dane blew out a sigh and reached for Stella's hand again. She always calmed him, always kept him focused on what was important. For nearly two decades, Dane and Ethan had wanted to get back at Robert for taking their legacy from them. Dane had reclaimed the resort in Montana, and now it was Ethan's turn. Then they planned on ruining Robert for good.

Yet now his reckless, playboy brother was veering off course, and Dane couldn't do much about the mess his twin was in.

"Listen," Ethan started in a calmer tone. "I had no clue who Harper was until this morning. She was just the woman I was having a fling with. I found out she was pregnant yesterday. Once my investigator told me who she was, I moved on that information. I'm not making apologies."

No, Ethan would never apologize. Not for this and not for closing in on himself when they lost their mother. Dane had needed his brother, had needed *someone* to seek comfort with during the hardest time in his life.

But Ethan hadn't been there. Not emotionally, anyway. Then Robert had stolen their financial stability and disappeared. Ethan had enlisted in the military, and Dane figured he might as well, too. Where else did he have to go? At least the military would provide a unit and stability.

"Now what?" Dane asked.

Stella wrapped her arms around him and laid her head on his shoulder. He loved this woman. He'd found her when he least expected to find anyone. He'd been so set on grabbing Mirage with both hands and never letting go.

But Stella had stepped into his path, and somehow he'd managed to get everything he hadn't even realized he wanted.

"Oh, wait." Dread hit Dane hard. "She doesn't know you hate her father, does she?"

"She's not aware of our history, no."

Dane let out a string of curses that had Stella smacking his chest.

"You know this not going to end well for you," Dane added.

"I'll get Mirage. That's what matters."

Dane snorted. "You don't mean that."

His brother sighed heavily on the other end. "No, I don't. I'm trying to keep my focus on the end result, but someone is going to get hurt, and now that all of this is in motion, all I can do is try to take the brunt of the blow when it happens."

Dane felt sorry for Ethan. For the first time in... well, ever, Ethan was feeling the ramifications of his actions, and Dane was truly worried.

Someone was going to get hurt, but Dane couldn't help but wonder if they were all going to feel the backlash from this series of events.

Harper stared over the various marble designs. All were in the same price point, all were equally stunning and all would make a killer impact in the lobby of Mirage.

But she couldn't decide.

She also couldn't stop thinking of Ethan's ridiculous half-assed proposal and her reply. What was she thinking? Sure, she could come up with some very necessary ground rules, but then what? Were they just going to play house and raise a baby like they were a happily married couple without having any kind of relationship beyond physical compatibility and a business agreement?

Sex could only take them so far. At some point, they'd have to actually do things together if they wanted this to succeed for the sake of the baby.

And how archaic did that sound? Was he just marrying her because of the baby? He'd made valid points of how they were both workaholics and they understood each other, but Harper had always envisioned marrying for love. Call her old-fashioned, but she truly believed there was a man out there for her.

Ignoring the marble slats on the desk, Harper pulled out her cell and brought up her texts.

Then she dropped her phone onto the desk and closed her eyes.

This wasn't the first time she'd started to message her sister for advice. In the past several months, Harper couldn't count how many times she'd started to call or text. How did she deprogram herself from that? Would there come a time when it would just click into place that this was her new normal? That there was no family to go to for advice?

Her mother had already stated that she'd raised her kids and now it was her turn to live. Her father was...well, not very loving.

Who did she have?

Harper truly hated this moment of self-pity, but she would like just one person to confide in. Someone she trusted to give her sound advice on what she should do.

Who knew when she came to Mirage over a month ago that she'd be in this situation? A baby, a proposal, a project of a lifetime. There was so much change, so much happening all at once, she didn't know where to direct her focus.

She flattened her hands on the desk, and the lighting caught the gold bracelet. At least she had that reminder of her sister. Little glimpses were warming, especially now when she needed to feel closer to Carmen.

The chime from her phone had Harper pulling from her thoughts and redirecting her attention to the new email. She quickly opened the message from her father's assistant.

The new budget was a go, and he'd even allotted an additional quarter of a million dollars. Well, that was certainly generous and shocking, but she didn't believe she'd go that far over.

Still, having a beautiful piece of property to renovate with virtually no top budget was a designer's dream come true. Carmen would have loved this.

This project meant so much for so many different reasons. Harper's giddiness rivaled that of a toddler on Christmas morning in a room full of unopened presents.

Harper shot off a quick reply and attached some of the files with her design sketches for the lobby, sample suites and dining areas. She doubted Robert would ever look at them, but she figured she'd show him anyway. He hadn't asked for an image yet.

Did he even care about the end result? Did he care she was here? She understood that he was a businessman first and a traveler second. She wasn't sure where father ranked in that list, but she hoped somewhere.

Every part of her wanted him to show up soon

so they could maybe have a nice dinner and discuss goals and the future. This pregnancy was going to be a new chapter in her life, and she wanted him to be part of it. Harper just wasn't sure that he would want the same.

She was well aware of what Ethan wanted, though.

Marriage. A business marriage. How unromantic could a proposal get? Because she was pretty sure this one was up there on the sucky proposal chart.

Still, she might just be falling for the charmer. She'd never admit such things. He didn't want love, and she couldn't exactly say what she felt toward him, but the emotion was more than like and more than just sexual.

So where did that leave her? On the verge of saying "I do" to a man she knew very little about in the hopes that they could build some future together? Were futures really built on heated beach flings and accidental pregnancies?

Harper sank down into the leather office chair and stared back at the marble samples. She couldn't even choose a shade of rock—how in the hell was she going to make a final commitment for the rest of her life?

Ten

"What am I missing? There has to be a subtle blue undertone for the calming effect. But what if it's too much?"

Ethan crossed his arms over his chest and listened to Harper mutter to herself as she stood at the desk and stared down at samples. He couldn't help but smile. She hadn't even noticed him. When he'd been about to knock, he'd been struck by how stunning she was standing there.

Oh, the punch of lust at the sight of her was nothing new, but the way she'd tipped her head and chewed on the tip of the pen was downright attractive. He admired a woman who got swept into her work. He'd already established that she was devoted, but seeing her so hands-on, so committed, was something he couldn't dismiss.

Then she'd started chatting to her work, and he didn't want to cut in. Sometimes he was a total gentleman. But she was just so adorable that he was afraid he'd start laughing in a minute—which meant it was time to announce himself. If she looked up and saw him seemingly laughing at her, the conversation would not go well.

"Am I interrupting?" he asked, tapping his knuckles on the door frame.

Harper jerked her attention to him, then shook her head. "Just having a staff meeting."

Ethan laughed and stepped on into her makeshift office. She'd told him where it was, but this was the first time he'd actually made it down here. He'd had no reason to, really. Up until now, his days had been his, his nights had been hers, but they'd always been in his penthouse.

He took a glance around the small space that wasn't much bigger than a storage closet. Actually, this used to be a storage closet. Ethan recalled the many times he'd visit Mirage with his mother when he'd been younger and how he'd explored and learned every inch of it. She was so proud to show him the place that would one day be his. She'd done the same with Dane at Mirage in Montana.

Which was why he and Dane were stopping

at nothing to make all of this right. Their mother had had a plan for the things she loved most in the world—her sons and her resorts. And just because she was taken from this earth all too soon didn't mean they shouldn't see her vision through.

Marble slats covered the old, narrow desk. She had a laptop open to a mock design of the lobby. Ethan whistled.

"That looks amazing," he stated, circling the desk to get a closer view. "This isn't your sister's design."

Harper came in beside him, her shoulder brushing against his. "How do you know?" she asked. "You never met Carmen."

"I don't know," he murmured, his eyes studying every last detail. "There's something about the blues here that make it seem like you're walking on water, but it's so subtle and calming. But then you throw in a subtle punch of red with the flowers and that's just so you."

"That's what I wanted."

"The lighting is magnificent," he went on. "You can't see the fixtures, but they're perfect. And that island of fresh flowers in all white…brilliant."

"The lobby is the first thing guests see when they check in," she stated. "I mean, I know they look on-line for every available picture, but once they step inside after traveling to get here, I want them to just let all the stress and exhaustion fade away. I want to transform them to another world where everyday problems cease to exist."

Ethan turned his attention to her as she spoke. Her eyes never wavered from the screen as she explained her reasoning behind such extravagance.

"You've managed to capture everything," he told her.

Harper blinked, turning her eyes to his. "Well, I don't know about that. I'm sure there will be stumbling blocks, and issues will come to light that I'm not thinking of right now."

"That comes along with any business plan," he replied. "The important thing is to know how to handle the hardships when they come along."

Harper pursed her lips. "I don't plan on failing."

"I have no doubt you'll make this a complete success."

She offered him a smile that did something unfamiliar to his…heart?

No. That was absurd. His heart wasn't involved in any of this. Well, *part* of his heart was very involved in all of this—the portion that belonged to his mother, to her memories and legacy and the future she'd promised him.

"I think if I can get through losing my sister, I can get through a bump in the road of this project," she told him.

Ethan wanted her to remain focused on her rea-

"FAST FIVE" READER SURVEY

Your participation entitles you to:
* ✳ 4 Thank-You Gifts Worth Over $20!

Complete the survey in minutes.

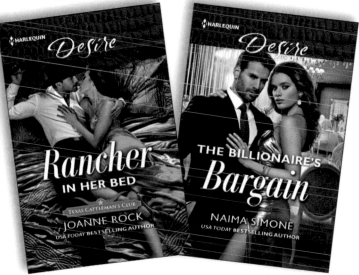

Get 2 FREE Books

See inside for details.

Dear Reader,

Since you are a lover of our books, your opinions are important to us... and so is your time.

That's why we made sure your **"FAST FIVE" READER SURVEY** can be completed in just a few minutes. Your answers to the five questions will help us remain at the forefront of women's fiction.

And, as a thank-you for participating, we'd like to send you **4 FREE THANK-YOU GIFTS!**

Enjoy your gifts with our appreciation,

Pam Powers

To get your
4 FREE THANK-YOU GIFTS:

✻ Quickly complete the "Fast Five" Reader Survey
and return the insert.

"FAST FIVE" READER SURVEY

1	Do you sometimes read a book a second or third time?	○ Yes	○ No
2	Do you often choose reading over other forms of entertainment such as television?	○ Yes	○ No
3	When you were a child, did someone regularly read aloud to you?	○ Yes	○ No
4	Do you sometimes take a book with you when you travel outside the home?	○ Yes	○ No
5	In addition to books, do you regularly read newspapers and magazines?	○ Yes	○ No

YES! I have completed the above Reader Survey. Please send me my 4 FREE GIFTS (gifts worth over $20 retail). I understand that I am under no obligation to buy anything, as explained on the back of this card.

225/326 HDL GNQC

FIRST NAME   LAST NAME

ADDRESS

APT.#   CITY

STATE/PROV.   ZIP/POSTAL CODE

READER SERVICE—Here's how it works:

Accepting your 2 free Harlequin Desire® books and 2 free gifts (gifts valued at approximately $10.00 retail) places you under no obligation to buy anything. You may keep the books and gifts and return the shipping statement marked "cancel." If you do not cancel, about a month later we'll send you 6 additional books and bill you just $4.55 each in the U.S. or $5.24 each in Canada. That is a savings of at least 13% off the cover price. It's quite a bargain! Shipping and handling is just 50¢ per book in the U.S. and $1.25 per book in Canada*. You may cancel at any time, but if you choose to continue, every month we'll send you 6 more books, which you may either purchase at the discount price plus shipping and handling or return to us and cancel your subscription. *Terms and prices subject to change without notice. Prices do not include sales taxes which will be charged (if applicable) based on your state or country of residence. Canadian residents will be charged applicable taxes. Offer not valid in Quebec. Books received may not be as shown. All orders subject to approval. Credit or debit balances in a customer's account(s) may be offset by any other outstanding balance owed by or to the customer. Please allow 3 to 4 weeks for delivery. Offer available while quantities last.

▲ If offer card is missing write to: Reader Service, P.O. Box 1341, Buffalo, NY 14240-8531 or visit www.ReaderService.com ▲

BUSINESS REPLY MAIL

FIRST-CLASS MAIL   PERMIT NO. 717   BUFFALO, NY

POSTAGE WILL BE PAID BY ADDRESSEE

READER SERVICE
PO BOX 1341
BUFFALO NY 14240-8571

NO POSTAGE
NECESSARY
IF MAILED
IN THE
UNITED STATES

sons for doing this, because ultimately, this remodel would carry over into his ownership.

"Tell me more about Carmen," he commanded, easing his hip on the edge of her desk, meeting her eye level.

Harper stared for a moment before she crossed her arms over her chest. He wondered if she did this as a coping mechanism to hold in the hurt. He'd had to break himself of just that after his mother had passed.

"She was bright. Not only smart, but she just beamed everywhere she went. It was impossible to see her and not smile."

He could say the same exact thing about Harper, but he didn't interrupt.

"She had a big heart and an even bigger out-going spirit." Harper let out an adorable laugh. "She was always dragging me to parties or out to dinner with her friends. She'd do anything to get me out of the house."

Ethan reached for her hands and gripped them on his lap. "You didn't get out much?"

Harper shrugged, glancing down to their joined hands. "Let's just say I didn't have the confidence my sister did."

She smiled and glanced back up to him. "I was always overweight and shy in school. My sister was the popular cheerleader and homecoming queen. I was so proud to be her sister, but I never felt like I measured up."

"That's absurd," he replied before thinking. "What does size have to do with anything at all?"

Harper tipped her head. "That's so easy for a man to say. Being a plus-size girl in high school is not the funnest of times. Changing for gym class while trying to hide that roll over your pants or going shopping for prom dresses when your friends are grabbing their size twos and fours while I'm over there whispering for an eighteen."

Ethan listened but didn't hear pain in her voice. He heard strength and bravery.

"And what made you see yourself differently?" he asked, tugging her farther to stand between his legs.

"I got out of school, where there was too much competition to be perfect," she told him. "My mother started traveling around the world, and my sister and I grew even closer. I realized I have one life, and spending each day questioning what other people thought wasn't the way I wanted to live."

Ethan released her hands and reached for her hips. "That's a pretty smart revelation."

"Well, I kept telling myself that, but it took a while before I started to actually believe the words." Harper rested her hands on his shoulders, the tips of her thumbs brushing along his neck. "My sister constantly urged me to get out more and more, so over the years I went when she asked. Coming here was strictly for work."

"You don't usually travel alone?" he asked. "Get away and just take vacations to treat yourself?"

"I never have. Carmen and I would go places, but this is the first time I've gone anywhere by myself. I was packing to come here and saw that skimpy red bikini."

Harper laughed again and sighed. "Carmen bought me that last summer, and I refused to wear it. I tried it on, and she kept telling me how good I looked and told me not to hide a killer body."

"I like your sister."

Harper smacked his shoulder. "You like boobs, so don't act like it was the bikini."

"Why can't I appreciate both?" he asked.

"Anyway," she went on, rolling her eyes. "Circling back to my sister. She's the reason I've evolved so much, and she's the reason I'm here. She started this company and asked me to join her, having more faith in me than I did in myself."

"Sounds like she had faith in you about everything."

Harper nodded, biting her lower lip as her chin quivered just a touch. "She did. I guess I just feel lost without her. It's got me second-guessing my decisions here."

"She wouldn't want that."

"No," Harper agreed. "She wouldn't."

"So why are you doing this to yourself?"

With a shrug, she held his gaze. "Because I don't have anyone to tell me otherwise."

Ethan released her hips and framed her face. "Then consider me that someone. You're brilliant, you're talented and you're going to turn this resort into something magical."

Tears filled her eyes. "You sound so sure," she murmured.

Ethan was positive. There wasn't a doubt in his mind that she'd have Mirage on the bucket list of everyone from suburban housewives to A-list celebrities. Mirage of Sunset Cove would be the place everybody flocked to when they wanted to escape.

And it would be all his.

"I'm positive," he insisted, easing forward just enough to slide his lips over hers.

He couldn't resist her, wasn't even going to try. There was something here that pulled him closer and closer into her world. Not the baby and not the fact she was Robert's daughter. There was a storm brewing inside him.

And he was scared as hell.

Ethan nipped at her bottom lip and smoothed his thumb over the dampness as he eased back.

"Let me see what you're torn between here," he offered. "I know a thing or two about design."

Harper licked her lips, tempting him to clear this desk with one swoop and spread her out over it. But the businessman in him took over. He wanted to know about final decisions, and if he was careful, he might just be able to assist in achieving the end result he wanted.

Blowing out a breath, Harper stepped back and gestured to the samples beside his hip.

"I like them all," she stated. "I can envision each one of those in the lobby, and none of them are wrong."

Ethan came to stand and turned his attention toward the marble slats. He studied each one and then glanced to her screen, where the design layout was still pulled up.

"Which one do you think?" she asked after a bit.

Ethan shoved his hands in his pockets and shook his head. "I want to know your first instinct."

"I told you I love them all," she reiterated.

"No. When you look at them, if you're honest, you're drawn to one."

He watched as she glanced over them, her eyes lingering on the slat with a subtler swirl pattern—the exact option he would've chosen.

"This one was the first one I pulled when I initially asked for the samples," she said, smoothing her hand over the flawless piece.

"Don't doubt yourself," he told her. "You've got this. Not just the flooring, but the entire project. Do you think Carmen would've asked you to join her brainchild had she not had faith in your capabilities?"

Harper smiled. "You're scolding me like she used to."

"Well, maybe someone needs to move into her old spot," he declared. "Speaking of, you never gave me an actual answer to the proposal."

"No, I didn't."

Oh, she was such a tease. He loved every bit of her sass and knew they'd make a great team. He just needed her to officially say yes.

"How could a marriage between us work?" she asked.

"First of all, neither of us likes to fail or admit defeat, so we're already a determined pair."

Ethan moved around her, adjusted the desk chair and placed his hands on her shoulders, easing her down.

"What are you doing?" she asked as her butt hit the seat, her eyes wide as she stared up at him.

"You seem tired," he stated. "I didn't want you passing out on me."

"I seem tired?" she repeated. "Maybe it's because my nights are consumed with a man who has more stamina than a triple-crown racehorse."

Ethan let out a bark of laughter. "I don't know that I'm that active, but I'll take it as a compliment."

"You would," she murmured. "Anyway, I'm not passing out. I've never passed out in my life."

"You've never been pregnant before, either."

She pursed her lips, apparently irritated that she had no comeback.

"Good. Now, circling back around." Ethan rested his hands on the arms of her chair, stared into those dark eyes and moved on. "The second reason we'd make this marriage work is because we both value family and would want the best for our baby."

"What if I want to marry for love?" she volleyed back.

Ethan jerked back. "Have you ever been in love?"

Harper seemed to roll the question through her head before she answered. "No."

"Can you think of a valid reason, other than love, not to marry me?"

She stared at him and smoothed a hand over her abdomen. "Well, we've only known each other just over a month. I'm not sure how stable our future can be since you started our fling based on a bikini."

"A move I don't regret, by the way."

She rolled her eyes as she went on. "I don't know where we'd live or how I'd carry on Two Sisters Design if I had to move."

"I'd never ask you to give up your life or your dreams," he told her. "Neither of us will have to give up anything. We can work together, we can live in your home or buy a new place. I'm flexible since I travel so much anyway, so our home can be anywhere that's good for your business."

"I can't believe I'm seriously considering this," she muttered.

"I can't believe you're taking so long to agree to what would be a perfect solution."

Harper moved farther away, which wasn't far since the room was so small. She continued to stare at him, and he could only imagine the war she was waging with herself. There wasn't a doubt in Ethan's mind that she'd agree. He *needed* her to agree. He liked things neat and tidy when it came to business, and whether he liked it or not, Harper was part of this scheme. Never in his life did he drop an innocent into his plans, but fate had other ideas for both of them now.

Trying to keep Harper safe from harm was impossible, but he planned on doing his best to protect her as much as he could. He wanted to be there for her once she found out the monster her father was. There was no way she could know already. Someone like Harper wouldn't associate with the likes of Robert Anderson if she didn't have to—her indignation on his behalf when he'd told her about his stepfather had made that clear.

And since she hadn't even connected with her biological father until she was in her early twenties, it was understandable that she didn't know him well enough to see past his respectable veneer. Ethan hated to be the one to have to reveal what a bastard Robert was.

It was best she found out now, though. Robert didn't deserve Harper, and he sure as hell didn't deserve a relationship with his grandchild.

"All right," Harper finally said. "I'll marry you."

Ethan released a sigh of relief. Everything was falling into place, and he was one more step closer to obtaining everything he wanted…and more.

Eleven

Harper's belly continued to roll, and she wasn't sure if it was morning sickness that had moved into the evening hours or if she was still reeling from agreeing to Ethan's marriage proposal yesterday.

Either way, she was out of her element with both new chapters in her life.

And her father was due here soon. Would he even take interest in the fact he was going to be a grandfather or have a son-in-law? He'd barely grasped the whole fatherhood role, so she highly doubted he'd be very interested in donning the other two hats.

Harper eased into the bright blue floor-length gown and wondered how much longer until her waistline expanded. She never thought she'd be excited about getting larger, but she was. She wanted to see that round belly, wanted to embrace the magical gift that only a woman could experience.

The shimmering material caught the light as she turned side to side in the mirror. This dress was going to make Ethan's eyes bug out of his head. Another magical spell women possessed. Men thought they were so tough, so strong, but in reality, a woman could render them speechless with such simple things…like a killer dress. Or a red bikini.

Tonight Mirage was hosting a mock casino night, and she wanted to go mingle with the guests, maybe even get a feel for what some of them thought about the resort. You could learn quite a bit just from small talk with people, and if she simply acted like any other guest, she might just discover the likes and dislikes the others felt toward Mirage.

While her plan for renovations was pretty well set, she could adjust if necessary…especially with that generous added budget.

She'd spent last night in his penthouse…their first night since agreeing to stay together. They were starting this new life since she'd agreed to marry him.

The words still felt so foreign running through her mind. But she didn't regret telling Ethan yes. Marriages were built on much less than what they had, as he'd pointed out.

Harper grabbed her small gold clutch from the dresser and slid her room key and red lip gloss inside. With a snap of the closure, she tucked the accessory beneath her arm and headed for the door.

The second she opened it, Harper let out a squeal and jumped back.

"Sorry." Ethan stood there, fist raised and ready to knock. "Perfect timing."

Harper put a hand to her chest and pulled in a shaky breath. "Perfect timing for a heart attack?"

Ethan's eyes raked over her from head to toe and back up again. Harper's heart beat fast for a totally new reason now. He stood before her in an all-black tux, looking both classy and dangerous. That messy hair had been calmed, but the stubble along his jaw lingered, as if he needed just that bit of scruff to remain true to himself.

"Have I told you today how sexy you are?" he murmured, taking a step forward and backing her into her suite.

"You don't say the words, no," she replied, suddenly feeling like prey…and she had to admit she didn't mind. "But I get the gist by how you look at me. And touch me."

Ethan took another step until he came within inches of her. His hands rested on her hips, and he tugged her pelvis to line up with his. The dress was clearly a hit.

"Let me rectify that," he growled. "You're the

sexiest woman I've ever met. You're the sexiest fiancée I've ever had."

Harper laughed and flattened her hands against his chest. "Have there been other fiancées?"

Ethan eased closer, grazing his lips ever so softly against hers. "You're the only one."

Oh, how she wished he truly meant those words. Was she naive and foolish to want more from him than a businesslike marriage?

"It still doesn't feel like a real engagement," she murmured. "I've never been engaged, though, so I'm not sure what it's supposed to feel like."

Ethan released her and smiled. "Something else I plan on fixing."

Confused, Harper stared at him as he reached into his pocket and pulled out a small box. Breath caught in her throat and her gaze went from the box to his cocky smile.

"I hope you like it." He slowly lifted the lid to reveal a bright emerald-cut ruby nestled in a simple gold band. "It's not a traditional diamond, but we don't exactly have a traditional relationship…if there is such a thing."

Harper couldn't believe the stunning ring he presented to her. Never in her life had she expected him to get an engagement ring. The thought hadn't crossed her mind.

"If you don't like it, we can get something else,"

he added. "This was my mother's ring. I just figured since family was important to both of us—"

"It's perfect, but how did you get it here so fast? I assume you don't travel with your mother's jewelry."

Ethan smiled and shook his head. "I pay my assistant extremely well to go above and beyond."

She reached for the ring, but he pulled back and took it out. Ethan grabbed her hand and slid the ring on her finger. Harper felt the familiar sting of tears, and she didn't even try to hold them back.

"Are you sure you want to waste this on me?" she asked, admiring the ring and thankful it fit. "I mean, shouldn't you save this for someone… I don't know. Special?"

Ethan squeezed her hand. "You're the mother of my child. I'd say that makes you pretty damn special."

A tear slipped out, followed by another. Ethan swiped the pads of his thumbs across her cheeks and eased forward. Harper gripped his wrists as he framed her face and slid his lips over hers.

Ethan eased her backward, farther into the suite, all the while slowly making love to her mouth.

Harper's body tingled with anticipation. The silky lining of the gown caressed her bare skin like a lover's caress.

They weren't going to make it to the party downstairs…not while they were busy having their own private celebration.

Harper's dress hit the floor in seconds with a flitter of hands and lips working their way over her body. She stepped out of the puddled material as Ethan continued to walk her backward, leading her toward the bedroom.

But then he turned her in the hall and pressed her back against the wall. Harper wasn't about to have another repeat of the other night in the kitchen when she was bare and he remained clothed. She wanted him, all of him, and she wanted him now.

While his mouth continued trailing up her neck and back to her lips, Harper reached between them and slid his jacket off his broad shoulders. Then she went to work on each little button of his tuxedo shirt until she rid him of that garment, too.

Finally, she eased her fingertips over each taut muscle of his pecs and abs. Ethan growled and reached around to cup her backside as her hands ventured to the top of his pants. She hurriedly unfastened, unzipped and seesawed his pants down his hips.

Ethan took a step back, releasing her as he toed off his shoes and stepped from his pants and boxer briefs. Then he was on her again, gripping her waist and lifting her to meet him.

Instinctively, Harper wrapped her legs around him and was even more turned on by his strength, his hunger and his clear need to have her before they even reached the bedroom.

"Harper," he murmured in her ear as he joined their bodies.

She clung to his shoulders, dropping her head back against the wall. One of his hands rested beside her head while the other held on to her backside. His hips jerked, making Harper cry out. Every single time with Ethan was magnificent and unlike anything she'd ever experienced.

He whispered things to her, nothing she could make out, not when her entire mind and body were absorbing all of the tantalizing emotions.

The swirl of her climax spiraled through her, hitting her fast and hard. Harper bit down on her lip and shut her eyes, wanting to hold every single moment of this bliss inside her without allowing any to escape.

"Harper."

The demand had her jerking her attention to Ethan, whose face was a breath from hers. His body had stilled as hers ceased trembling. She'd shut her eyes, her lashes fanning over her cheeks.

"Look at me," he demanded.

Harper stared into those captivating eyes. Only the light from the main living area filtered down the hallway, leaving half of his face in the dark.

The intensity of his gaze had her wondering what his thoughts were. Was he feeling more for her than lust and camaraderie? Was he ready to take this beyond sex and a business-type marriage?

The flash of vulnerability and emotions vanished from his expression just as quickly as she'd seen them. Ethan started moving once again, but he kept his attention all on her.

Harper threaded her fingers through the hair at the nape of his neck and jerked him in for a kiss. She wanted every part of him he was willing to give...and more.

Ethan opened for her, inviting her lips, just as his body jerked and his hand on her tightened. She swallowed his cry of pleasure and gave a slight tug on his hair.

When he lifted his head, Harper watched as the wave of passion swept over his face. There was something so intimate, so bonding about holding the stare of someone during their most vulnerable moment.

Gradually, Ethan's grip on her lessened as he leaned forward and dropped his head onto her shoulder. The warm breath that hit her bare skin had her shivering and trailing her fingertips up and down his back.

If they could stay like this, maybe she could believe just for a moment that he cared for her the way she desired, the way she'd dreamed of someone loving her. Could he ever? Would he eventually want a deeper connection? She thought she'd seen a glimpse of something in his eyes earlier...but maybe it had just been wishful thinking.

Slowly, Ethan released her. Harper straightened out her legs and dropped them to the floor. Her muscles protested, and she held on to his biceps.

"Not too steady?" he asked.

Harper shook her head. "Give me a second."

Ethan scooped her up in his arms. "I've got you."

Harper wrapped her arms around his neck and rested her head on his shoulder. No matter how independent, how strong-willed any woman was, when a man pulled the ultimate romantic move, it was time to settle in and enjoy the ride.

She only hoped this would last longer and grow to mean more, because she couldn't have a one-sided relationship. She deserved more.

Twelve

"You look good wearing that ring."

Ethan crossed his arms behind his head and admired Harper as she walked bare, save for the ruby ring and the gold bracelet she always wore, into the adjoining bath.

"Do you think we missed the entire party?" she asked, grabbing a short red robe from the back of the door.

That woman made the color red look damn good.

Ethan laughed. "I'm pretty sure the party wound down a couple hours ago."

Harper pursed her lips as she knotted the tie at

her waist. "Hmm... I was looking forward to the casino night. It sounded fun."

"There will be other fun theme nights," he assured her. "I believe next week there will be a Mardi Gras party in the courtyard."

She adjusted the V on her robe and sighed. "I suppose I could order a mask to match my dress. It's a shame to let it go to waste."

"Oh, it wasn't wasted," he affirmed. "I thoroughly enjoyed you in it."

With hands propped on her hips and head tipped to the side, Harper offered him a wide grin that hit him straight in the heart.

But his heart couldn't get involved. He hadn't allowed his heart to get involved with anyone since he was a teenager. Whatever he was feeling had to do with the anticipation and anxiety surrounding the baby, the engagement and the reunion with Robert.

But there was a moment in the hallway, a sliver of a second when he'd nearly let his guard down. He couldn't risk letting Harper in completely. Not until this entire mess was sorted out and all the lies dealt with. She deserved better, and he would make damn sure she got it.

He only prayed she didn't want to completely leave him after this was all out in the open. Would she listen to his side? Would she understand why he'd gone to such great lengths for revenge and why he'd kept the truth from her once he realized who she was?

"Tell me about your mother."

Harper's demand pulled him straight from his thoughts. "What brought that up?"

With a shrug, she crossed to the side of the bed he lay on and eased down next to his hip. Ethan shifted and settled his hand on her lap.

"You mentioned her passing, and you're protective of me, of this baby. I just figure she must have been an amazing woman to raise such a caring son."

Ethan wasn't sure how to put into words how amazing his mother had been. There wasn't a day that went by that he didn't miss her or wish he had her back.

"She was a single mother who raised my brother, Dane, and me the best she could," he started. "She inherited a good chunk of money from her father, and she invested it into opening two businesses. Her ultimate goal was to pass those down, one for Dane and one for me."

"Sounds like a smart woman." Harper rested her hand over his. "So how did you end up with the nightclubs? That wasn't her business, was it?"

Looking back, his life was a complicated mess, and he couldn't divulge the entire truth right now. Guilt pumped through him. He wanted to tell her, though. He wanted Harper to know the man Robert was.

Ethan was still trying to wrap his mind around the fact Harper was involved at all—even if it was by default. He didn't like it, he wanted to somehow remove her from the equation, but that was impossible.

Robert would be here soon. He had to tell her.

It was still such a mind-boggling fact that Robert could produce anything good, yet here Harper was— the best thing that had happened to him in a long, long time.

"Ethan?" Harper patted his arm, pulling his thoughts back to the sexy woman at his side. "Are you going to tell me about your mysterious past?"

Which part did he start with? There were so many layers to him, so much he hadn't divulged to anyone. But he was coming to realize that Harper was special. He hadn't lied when he'd told her as much. Something churned deep inside him. He couldn't put a label on the emotion and was terrified to even try.

"Like I told you before, after my mother passed, my stepfather stole our inheritance, and the businesses were transferred to his name by some slick, underhanded attorney. Dane and I had no idea until after all the legal paperwork had been signed."

"I still can't believe anyone would do that," she replied. "Especially to grieving kids."

If she only knew...

Damn it. He absolutely hated every bit of this. She was a victim, just as much as he had been. Harper was too innocent, too sweet to be wrapped up in this mess, and she had no clue the explosion that was on the verge of blowing up in her face.

Ethan didn't know how, but he'd do everything in his power to block the pain from reaching her.

"We were seniors in high school, so we were almost graduated," he went on. "We both ended up enlisting in the army. Something shifted with us when Mom died. I take the blame for that."

Harper turned and lifted her knee up onto the bed as she leaned toward him. "You can't take all the blame. Every failed relationship is two-sided."

"We didn't exactly fail," he amended. "But I closed in on myself. I didn't know how to handle all that grief, so I turned to liquor and sex as an easy escape. It hurt to look at my brother, because I didn't want to see that mirror image of pain."

Harper flatted her hand over his chest, the warmth of her tender touch giving him the courage to continue. Even nearly twenty years later, the ache of losing his mother and the tragic failure of his relationship with his brother all those years was almost unbearable.

"We drifted apart and I let it happen," he continued, swallowing the lump of emotion in his throat. "But as time passed, we agreed on one thing. We wanted to take down the bastard who stole everything from us when we were most vulnerable. It took time, it took patience, but we knew once we were powerful and wealthy enough, nothing would stand in our way."

"Good for you guys," Harper cheered. "He deserves to pay. But how did you come to be a nightclub owner?"

He let the conversation shift, but soon she would discover the truth…and it had to be him that revealed it to her. If she found out any other way, she'd hate him, and he couldn't stand the thought of Harper looking at him with anything other than infatuation and desire in her eyes.

"After the service, I was still lost. I had no clue what I was going to do with my life. I had little money, just what I'd saved from the army."

Harper's fingertips scrolled an invisible pattern over his chest, but her eyes remained locked on his. Did she even know she was silently reassuring him to go on? Did she have a clue that she was the balm he needed to rehash all of this?

"I was in San Diego and ended up at a bar." Ethan slid his hand over the tie on her robe. "I'd been there before when I'd been home on leave.

I've always loved that city. The bartender recognized me, we got to talking, sharing our veteran stories, and the next thing I knew, he was making me a partner in business. He had that bar and was looking to open another in LA and in Boston."

"That's rather lucky," she told him with a grin. "And you're trying to distract me."

She glanced down to her waist, where her robe had come apart. Ethan smiled as he slid the material even farther from her lush body.

"Did you ever think that you're the one who distracts me?" he retorted. "You have some power over me that I can't explain."

That was the truest thing he'd ever told her.

Ethan's hands grazed her belly, and the reality of a baby—*his baby*—being right there reminded him exactly what was at stake. Everything. His future was riding on Robert, on Harper, on himself.

"So are we done with story time?" she asked, easing up to straddle his lap.

"I'd say we've talked enough."

Because he still wasn't ready to tell her the last piece of the puzzle. Tomorrow. He would tell her tomorrow. He wanted one more night in this fantasy land where everything was all right and there was no outside force that could potentially ruin the way she looked at him.

Because something was happening between

them that had nothing to do with the baby and nothing to do with sex. Now Ethan just needed to figure out what the hell to do with that knowledge and how he should deal with these raw feelings that could ultimately destroy this good thing.

Ethan slid the crucial documents back into the safe in the walk-in closet of his penthouse suite. He'd spent last night in Harper's bed, but today she was moving all of her things into his space.

Before that happened, he wanted to make sure everything was tucked away, out of her line of sight.

Ethan had several statements he planned on using for blackmail against Robert should Robert not give up the property willingly. There were papers regarding tax fraud and money laundering—just a sampling of charges Ethan would threaten.

He sincerely hoped Robert would just man up and do the right thing, but as that was highly unlikely, Ethan had a foolproof backup plan. He wouldn't have come here and wouldn't have collaborated with Dane if he wasn't one hundred percent certain they were ready to take down Robert.

Once the resort was rightfully signed over to Ethan, he had every intention of turning Robert in to the authorities. There were two other copies of all of these documents. Dane had a set and so did Ethan's attorney.

Robert should be arriving in the next few days. Ethan wanted everything put away and not a trace of the damning evidence for Harper to see. Not until he had a chance to tell her everything.

Which would be today. He'd already told her he wanted to meet her around lunchtime to discuss something important. He hated having to be the one to tell her that her father was a manipulating bastard, but if he didn't, she'd find out soon enough and likely the hard way...like when Robert duped her for his own selfish reasons.

The thought of Robert stealing anything from Harper was an added layer of motivation for Ethan to take full control over all of this and get ahead of the game.

Ethan punched in the code on the safe and stepped from the closet into his bedroom. He glanced at the time on his phone and blew out a sigh. He had about an hour to kill before meeting up with Harper.

There was nothing with his clubs or potential investment property in France that he could focus on right now. Nerves were getting the best of him, and he needed somewhere to channel all this restless energy.

He pulled up Dane's messages and shot off a text telling his brother that he was about to tell Harper the truth. He wasn't sure what sort of reply he was expecting from Dane, but Ethan wanted him to know what was going on. And he wished like hell his brother was here, but they would get together and celebrate once the deal was all done.

Once all of this was behind them, once the resorts were fully theirs and Robert was out of their lives for good, Ethan vowed to spend more time with his brother. If that meant flying to cold-as-a-polar-bear's-butt Montana, then so be it. He and Dane were both entering new chapters, important chapters, in their lives, and Ethan wanted them to grow together again. He wanted his child to know Dane. What better way to bridge their past and future relationships than with a fresh start and new life?

His cell vibrated in his hand, but when he glanced down, the screen showed a message from Harper.

Meet me in the lobby. I have a surprise.

A surprise? Well, if it was in the lobby then their clothes wouldn't be coming off. But what could she have for him? When did she have time to plan anything?

Something warmed inside him. He didn't know the last time anyone surprised him with anything. Certainly no woman. Harper was special, she was…

In the dark.

Ethan ignored the fear that crept up and threatened to strangle him. It was time to face her, and once she presented him with whatever surprise she had, he'd have to get her somewhere private and tell her the truth.

There was no more time.

Ethan made his way to his elevator, rehearsing in his head exactly how he'd break this news to her. Her reaction would likely be instant anger, but he needed to make her see his side of things. He needed to make her understand he'd truly had no clue who she was when he first approached her. But he should've, damn it. His investigators should've had Harper's name, age, address, hell, her favorite breakfast cereal in their research. But they'd given him nothing but the fact Robert had a daughter he rarely had dealings with.

A daughter Ethan was now engaged to and expecting a baby with.

Would she listen to him? Would she see the parallel between herself and his own mother and understand that he never wanted her to be hurt?

The elevator doors slid open, and Ethan was greeted by a bustling lobby. As he stepped out, he took in the well-dressed people he assumed belonged to a wedding party. The girls all wore pale pink dresses, and the men wore black pants and white button-down shirts. Ethan scanned a bit more until he spotted the beaming bride and groom near the fountain in the middle of the open lobby. The laughter and chatter were almost deafening to his ears.

His gaze traveled through the crowd as he made his way across the open lobby. The breeze from the ocean wafted in, but while the scent was typically a comforting one, given his love of the water and the beach, even that couldn't calm his nerves today.

Ethan circled the fountain, and there she was. Harper had on a beautiful white sundress that grazed the floor; her hair was down and all wild and curly. The juxtaposition of calm and chaos had his heart beating wildly.

This wasn't the first time she'd stolen his breath, but this might be the first time he couldn't ignore that niggle of something more stirring inside him. As much as he wanted to deny it, he was falling for her. How the hell had he let this happen?

She was talking to a man whose back was to Ethan, so he made his way over. Harper laughed at something, but then glanced over the man's shoulder and waved at Ethan.

The man turned around, and in that moment, Ethan's world came to a crashing halt as Robert Anderson met his gaze.

Every noise, every person, every single thing happening around him ceased to exist.

Ethan's past and his future had just collided in front of his face like a ticking bomb, and there was nothing he could do to dodge the explosion.

He was out of time.

Thirteen

Ethan clenched his fists at his sides as Robert Anderson had the audacity to not only hold his stare with all the confidence in the world, but to smile like the underhanded, devious bastard he was.

What an arrogant jerk.

"Ethan, come here. I want you to meet someone."

Harper extended her hand, inviting him over, but Ethan couldn't take his eyes off the devil himself. Robert's evil grin never faltered. It was like the man didn't have a care in the world, and he didn't seem one bit surprised to see his stepson.

"Ethan, this is my dad, Robert," Harper introduced them, oblivious to the tension. "Robert, this is Ethan. My fiancé."

Robert's bushy brows rose up. "Fiancé? Well, let me shake your hand."

Oh, hell no. Ethan shifted out of reach and wrapped a protective arm around Harper's waist. He wasn't about to touch that bastard and play nice.

"I had no idea Harper was dating," Robert stated, dropping his hand.

Clearly stepdaddy was going to pretend like he didn't know Ethan. Fine by him...for now. Harper still deserved the truth, but since they were standing in a lobby full of people—including a wedding party snapping candid photos—this was neither the time nor the place.

"We've been seeing each other for a while," Ethan stated, daring Robert to say something crude toward Harper.

Ethan might have lied by omission to her, but there was no way he'd let anyone treat her with anything less than respect.

Damn it. He should've told her the truth before now. He had no clue how everything had spiraled out of control, but now that it had, there was no option for him other than to face the fallout.

He didn't deserve her forgiveness, but he would be asking for it later anyway. He'd never begged for a damn thing in his life, but Harper was the exception to all of his usual rules.

"Robert owns Mirage," Harper said, her voice full of pride. "That's why this renovation project has been so important to me."

"He owns the resort?" Ethan questioned, feigning surprise. He wasn't sure how else to act and being blindsided didn't give him time to plan. "Well, that must be quite time-consuming." He finally turned to focus on Robert. "It's funny, though. I've been here over a month and this is the first I've seen you."

Robert's eyes narrowed slightly, just like Ethan recalled him doing when he'd gotten angry years ago. Like when Dane and Ethan had played harmless pranks that Robert never found humor in.

Apparently Robert wasn't amused now, either.

"I'm lucky that I'm free to come and go as I please," Robert finally replied.

Your luck is about to run out.

"I didn't know you would be here so soon," Harper told Robert. "I mean, I knew you were coming, but I thought you still had another few days with work."

Yeah, so did I.

Robert shrugged a shoulder. "Some things can wait. I wanted to see my daughter."

Ugh. The man dripped with a sliminess that Ethan didn't want near Harper or their child.

Robert hadn't aged well, which elated Ethan. The sixtysomething man had gotten pudgy around the middle, weathered in his face, with dark circles beneath his eyes. Apparently lying and deceiving people for a living didn't do good things for one's health. Shame that.

"Do you want to plan on dinner this evening?" Harper asked. "We have so much to catch up on, and I want you and Ethan to get to know each other."

Ethan literally had to bite back an instant refusal. A patient man was a smart man. That's how he'd come so far in his line of work. He'd waited for the right opportunities for everything and let the payoff be his reward.

He would wait and see what Robert said, because there was nowhere Harper would go in this resort that Ethan wouldn't be right by her side now. No way would he let Robert be alone with her. There was no telling what lies the man would tell her.

"Dinner sounds fabulous." Robert's eyes drifted to Ethan. "You'll join us."

Ethan sneered. "Wouldn't miss it."

Harper let out a little squeal of excitement. "This is great. I'll show you around and you can get a better idea of my plans in person. The crew will start next week, so you're just in time. How long will you be here?"

Robert glanced between the two and quirked his lips. "Not sure yet. I'm open to sticking around awhile."

Not if Ethan had any say about it. Robert had

better get his jet and pilot ready, because Ethan had every intention of getting this jerk out of here sooner rather than later.

If Robert wasn't ready to expose the fact they knew each other quite well, that might work to Ethan's benefit. He needed to talk to Harper without another opinion weighing in. His time had run out.

Every step from here on out would have to be more calculated than anything he'd ever done. Harper and this baby were his top priority, but he still had to get this resort.

Anything less than all of that was failure. And Ethan never failed.

"You were a little rude," Harper murmured as they stepped on to the elevator that would take them up to Ethan's penthouse. "I thought you'd be more excited about meeting my father."

Hadn't they discussed the importance of family? Surely he knew that she really wanted her family life to grow. She *needed* that comfort and stability in her life now more than ever.

"Was I?" Ethan questioned, lacing his hand in hers. "I wasn't trying to be. Maybe I was just caught off guard. I knew you were anxious for this project, but I didn't know your father was the owner."

The doors slid open to his penthouse…well, their penthouse, since her things were being moved in later today.

"I didn't want you to think I had this project simply because he took pity on me."

Ethan gripped her arm and pulled her to face him. Framing her face with his strong hands, he looked her directly in the eyes. A woman could so get lost in that dark gaze.

"I never would have thought that. Never," he repeated. "I've seen your samples. I've heard the passion in your voice when you discuss each detail. Maybe you had an advantage because he knew you, but if you weren't any good, you wouldn't be here. Robert wouldn't offer a pity job."

Harper rested her hands on his wrists at either side of her face. "You sound like you know him."

Ethan stared for a second before he shrugged. "I know people like him. I'm a businessman myself. We don't hire out mega jobs just to make someone feel good."

"I didn't want you to think—"

Ethan's lips covered hers for the briefest of moments before he eased back. "Stop. I think you're amazing. Your work ethic, your ideas, everything. Be proud of what you're doing. Confidence will get you everywhere."

That sounded like something Carmen would say. Maybe Ethan coming into her life had happened for a reason. Maybe he was exactly what she needed, exactly when she needed it.

Maybe she was falling too hard for him when

she wasn't completely sure if he could ever feel the same.

"I assume you didn't tell your dad about the baby."

Harper shook her head. "I thought I would wait. There was a lobby full of people, and it just didn't seem like the right time. I will at dinner."

She didn't know if her father would even care. She wanted him to take part in her child's life, especially considering he'd missed out on the first two decades of hers. But would he even want to? That was the question and one she feared the answer to.

"What's on your mind?" Ethan asked. "You have those worry lines between your brows."

"How do you know I'm worried? Those are just wrinkles."

Ethan kissed her forehead. "I know because they were there when you were looking at those marble samples and muttering to them."

Harper couldn't hold back her smile. "You think you know me so well."

His hands eased to her shoulders and gave a gentle squeeze. "I do know you. So, what are you worried about?"

"I just want him to be part of this baby's life," she admitted. "I didn't know who Robert was until I was twenty. I'd never met him. My mother was, and still is, quite the free spirit. She'd always told me my father wasn't interested in being a dad, so I let it drop. But then I just wanted to know. I wanted to give him the chance to see me for himself. So, Mom told me his name, and I looked him up. He didn't seem too thrilled to have a child when I met him, but we've been talking and getting together a few times a year ever since. I just wish…"

"You want a relationship."

Harper nodded. "I'm probably being foolish, I know. What grown woman begs a man for attention? I guess all the time we lost can't be made up, and I can't make him want to be a parent—much less a grandparent. Some people just aren't cut out for that job."

Ethan pulled her into his arms and wrapped her in his warmth, his strength. Harper rested her head against his chest, seeking his comfort, wanting so much more.

There was such a fine line between being hopeful and being realistic. She teetered on the brink of falling over into foolishness.

If Carmen were here, she'd be giving the best advice. Harper would give anything for one more conversation with her sister.

"I don't have the answers," he murmured against her ear. "But know that I'm here. This baby will know both parents love her."

Harper eased back, smirking, her brows raised. "Her?"

Ethan's mouth quirked into a grin. "I have a feeling the baby is a girl. I see her with your smile, your eyes. She's the most beautiful child."

Harper's heart swelled at hearing him talk about their child. He'd thought about the baby—he'd thought so much that he'd pictured her.

Stifling a yawn, Harper laid her head on his chest. Ethan's hands roamed up and down her back as he kissed her head.

"Go lie down," he urged. "I'll make sure you're not disturbed. That way you'll be refreshed for our dinner."

Harper smiled into his chest. "I don't know the last time I took a nap."

"Then I'd say you're long overdue." Ethan cupped her shoulders and pulled back. "Rest for as long as you want. You've got to stay healthy for our baby."

The baby. Yes. Maybe he only cared for her because of the baby. After all, that's the reason he proposed, right?

He placed another kiss on her forehead. "I have a few business things to tend to, but I'll make sure you're up in time to get ready for dinner."

Harper nodded. She was too tired to argue. These long nights were catching up to her, not to mention working during the day and the fatigue from pregnancy. Everything she'd read said that the first trimester was rough with nausea and the need to sleep all the time. Too bad she didn't have that luxury. Which was why she should take advantage of the opportunity to nap while she could.

"Wake me if you need me before," she told him.

"Don't worry about anything but getting some sleep."

As Ethan stepped back into the elevator and left her alone, part of her wondered if she should be completely open and honest with him. Should she tell him she was falling for him? If they were going to enter into marriage, she figured honesty was the best option.

After dinner, she vowed on another yawn as she crawled into Ethan's king-size canopy bed. Tonight would be one to remember with the two men in her life. She just wished she knew where she stood long term with both of them.

Fourteen

Ethan pounded on the wood door, clenching his other fist at his side.

A snick of the lock came a second before the door swung open to reveal a spacious ocean-view suite.

"Well, that took longer than I thought," Robert reprimanded. "I'm disappointed."

Ethan shoved his way into the suite. "I don't give a damn what you are. You're not staying here."

Robert closed the door and turned to face Ethan. He'd changed into some tacky tropical shirt and a pair of khaki pants. Just the sight of him made Ethan sick to his stomach, and it took every bit of his willpower not to punch that smug look off his face.

Spreading his arms out wide, Robert raised his brows. "Looks like I am."

Ethan had waited years for this moment. Years to make this bastard pay for everything he'd done— for destroying a legacy built by a single mother, for robbing two boys of their future.

But the dynamics had completely changed, and now so much more was at stake. Once again, Ethan's future and everything he'd come to care for were on the line.

"You're going to sign Mirage back to me." Ethan widened his stance, matched Robert's gaze and held his hands at his sides. "My attorney has the paperwork all drawn up. I have copies in my safe in my suite. I'll email a copy to whichever assistant of yours you want. But we're getting this deal done now. Today."

Silence settled heavy between them, but Robert made no move; he barely blinked. Ethan had no idea what reaction he'd expected. Perhaps mocking, arrogant laughter, but that's not the response he got. Robert continued to stare, and Ethan didn't know if the man was stunned speechless or weighing his attack.

Either way, Ethan was more than ready to tackle this beast.

"Is that why you're hanging all over my daughter?" Robert finally asked.

Ethan ground his teeth. "Don't act like you give a damn about her or anyone else. You care about yourself and your bank accounts, and that's it."

Ethan hoped to keep Harper out of this conversation as much as possible. Before Harper ever entered his life, Ethan had had one goal in mind. He hadn't lost sight of that—if anything he was more determined than ever to stake his claim and secure his mother's legacy so he could hand it down to his own child one day.

And Harper? She deserved to be rid of this piece of trash. She might not like that at first, because she had no clue who she was dealing with, but Ethan would protect her...at all costs.

"Why the interest in Harper?" Robert asked, quirking one silver brow. "Were you just passing the time? Waiting on me to arrive? If you're lying to her, deceiving her, that's no better than what you accuse me of."

Robert was trying to goad Ethan, but he wasn't having it. Guilt already laid a heavy blanket over him, and he was trying to make the right decisions from here on out. There were factors that were simply out of his control, much as he hated to admit it.

Now more than ever, he had people relying on him to make sure the right thing happened. This situation wasn't about him or Dane or even their mother right now. Harper and the baby were his future...his life.

Damn it. He couldn't lose her. He just…

He couldn't.

"You don't honestly think I'll just give you this property, do you?" Robert mocked with a sharp bark of laughter. "You're still a foolish kid. I did you and your brother a favor by taking these off your hands. What would kids have known about running a high-profile business like this?"

Ethan took a step forward, clenching his fists at his sides. "Our mother raised us in these resorts, and we knew every in and out of her work. We also would've trusted the managers she hired to work with us as we grew into our roles. But that's all in the past. Right here and now, I'm telling you that your time here is over. You're not keeping this place."

Robert studied him for a moment. "Is this because Dane has Mirage in Montana? Is that what this is about? You're jealous. You two were always in competition with each other."

Now it was Ethan's turn to laugh. "Now who's foolish? Dane and I have planned this for years. We're not in competition. We work together as a team, something you would never understand. We were never going to sit back and let you keep what belonged to us."

Robert's cheeks turned red as he puffed his chest with a big, deep breath. Every part of Ethan wanted to laugh at his stepfather trying to appear intimidating. That affect had come and gone years ago. Ethan couldn't wait to squash him and kick the bastard out of his life forever.

He only wished Dane were here to see all of this.

"And you think it's as easy as you just telling me what you want?" he retorted.

Before Ethan could reply, Robert circled him and went to the minibar to pour a drink.

"I'd offer you one, but you're not staying," Robert stated, tossing back the tumbler. "And as far as those documents, shove them up your—"

"Don't be so clichéd with your insults." Ethan shoved his hands in his pockets and glared across the room. "You've been laundering money and evading a good portion of your taxes for years. Well over a decade, actually."

Robert's eyes narrowed, but he remained silent... the one smart thing he'd done.

"I have proof, and with one word from me, I can have half a dozen law enforcement officials on you within minutes."

"You're bluffing," Robert accused. "You wouldn't do that to Harper."

No, he wouldn't purposely hurt Harper, but he wouldn't stop the inevitable, either. Everything that spiraled out of control now had been set in motion by Robert years ago.

Ethan took a step closer, then another, until the

only thing between them was that narrow bar. "Is that a risk you're willing to take?"

The muscles in Robert's jaw clenched as his grip around his empty tumbler tightened and his knuckles turned white. Ethan waited for him to toss the glass across the room, but the raging fit never came.

"Does Harper know you're blackmailing her father?"

"Harper doesn't know, because I haven't let her in on what a bastard you truly are…yet," Ethan tossed back. "But if you want to show all your hands, go see whose side she takes."

This part actually was a bluff—Ethan had no idea if she'd take his side. She likely would hate them both. He couldn't fault her for hating him, but even if she never wanted to see him again, he'd use every trick in his arsenal to make sure Robert didn't stay in her life, either. She deserved better than his poison.

"Oh, you think she's going to cling to your side when you reveal that I'm some big, bad monster?" Robert tossed back. "Sex doesn't mean a damn thing. That girl thrives on family. She doesn't care about money, which is why she won't make it far in her career. But that means she'll choose me over you any day."

Oh, she'd make it far, because she had common sense and a heart for serving others. She'd make it because she was headstrong and resilient.

And she'd choose him because he was giving her a new family.

It was on the tip of his tongue to mention the baby, but Ethan wasn't going to reveal that bit of news. He had to keep his family protected.

The reality of the situation hit him hard. Dane wasn't the only one Ethan was fighting for. Harper and their child were every bit his family now…and he cared for them.

He cared for Harper. His heart had entered the equation when he wasn't looking. He'd been so focused on this takeover and his revenge, he'd had no clue that he was falling for the innocent in all of this.

He wouldn't lose her. He refused to imagine his world without everything he wanted. There didn't have to be an either-or decision. Ethan wanted it all.

"I'm done here," Ethan stated. "You can either sign the papers or you can face prison time. Your future is in my hands, but I'm kind enough to give you a say."

Robert jaw eased back and forth as he seemed to give his options some consideration. Finally, he glanced down to his empty glass and gave a curt nod.

"You win."

Two words had never sounded sweeter. All these years, all the times he'd wondered if he would ever see this day, the moment had finally come.

But Ethan knew not to let his guard down so fast. Robert was a shark—he was ruthless and never one to just give in out of the kindness of his black heart.

"I'll have dinner with you and Harper and explain I have to leave on business," Robert went on.

Ethan cocked his head. "And I'm supposed to just take your word for this? You agreed pretty fast."

With a shrug, Robert refilled his glass. "A smart businessman knows when to cut his losses."

Maybe Robert was legitimately worried about the legalities of the situation...as he should be. Perhaps there was some conscience in there after all, and he realized this place never should've been his to begin with.

Ethan wasn't asking—he didn't want to stick around for any more chatter than necessary. But that didn't mean he wouldn't keep his radar up. Robert would pose a threat until all documents were signed and filed properly...or until the man was behind bars.

Now, if he could keep all of the ugliness away from Harper, find some way to explain without hurting her so they could both just move on. They could marry, raise their child, go about their careers and...

Yeah, it was the *and* part that terrified him. Who knew what tricks or traps Robert had waiting for them? There was no way the old bastard would go down this easily.

Ethan turned from the suite and let himself out.

One hurdle at a time.

Harper settled her hand at the crook in Ethan's arm as he led her into the Italian dining room. The resort had several restaurants, but this one was her favorite. She didn't even care that she could pound an entire plate of homemade ravioli in mushroom sauce. She planned on not only having that mouthwatering dish, but also the fresh-baked bread that practically melted in your mouth.

Her baby was going to love carbs.

Good thing she wore a flowy dress so she could enjoy her dinner without straining any seams. Harper had pulled out her fun red maxidress with a halter top and pulled her hair up on top of her head to stay cool. And since this was a special occasion, she'd also donned the blingiest earrings she had packed. The gold and diamonds hung in an intricate pattern and swayed with each step she took. The ruby on her finger and the gold bracelet on her wrist completed her look, and she'd never felt better.

Maybe it was the nap, maybe it was the fact she was about to go into carb overload…or maybe her happiness had everything to do with the man at her side and seeing her father again.

A renewed sense of hope blossomed within her, and Harper truly believed she could forge successful relationships with these two men. She had every reason in the world to want to make this happen. This baby gave her a new purpose, a reason to really fight for a familial future.

This day was already amazing, and she hadn't even discussed business with Robert yet. She couldn't wait to actually walk him through the rooms and the grounds and let him visualize each detail from her plan.

Excitement burst through her at the prospect of her ideas coming to life. The renovations would definitely take time, but in the end, the hard work would be worth it. Carmen would be proud, and that in and of itself was payment enough.

"I still say we should've stayed in the room and ordered room service," Ethan growled in her ear as they neared their table in the back. "I could show you how to properly eat Italian in bed."

Harper glanced his way. "Perhaps I'll let you do just that. Later," she vowed. "Right now, we're having dinner with my father. You already made me miss casino night because you couldn't leave the room."

He muttered something under his breath, but she couldn't make it out and she didn't get a chance to ask as they arrived at their table.

As soon as the hostess pulled out Harper's chair,

Robert came through the restaurant, headed straight toward them.

He extended his arms toward Harper and kissed her cheek in a very robotic manner that lacked the affection she desperately craved from him.

"I was running late," he told her. "I was afraid you'd be waiting."

"We just got here," Ethan replied.

Robert eased back and gestured toward the table. "Please, let's take a seat. I'm anxious to talk to you both."

Harper smiled as she settled next to Ethan. The waiter came over to fill their water glasses and take their drink orders. Harper admired the stunning floral arrangement of whites and greens when Robert's voice pulled her back.

Ethan had mentioned green to her just last night. He thought it might be a nice clean yet classy color scheme for one of the restaurants. Harper hadn't put that in her plans, but her decorative mind could see it in this open room. Whites and various shades green would be something to set the Italian restaurant apart from the rest of the resort.

Ethan was quite the little decorative assistant and handy to have in her corner.

"No wine?" Robert asked. "Last time we met up, you raved about a cab that you loved. Wine is always a perfect accessory to Italian cuisine."

Harper bit her bottom lip and darted her gaze

to Ethan. "Well, we're not only engaged, but we're also having a baby."

Robert's reaction was not one she'd thought she'd see. Granted, she wasn't sure what she'd expected, but maybe some semblance of happiness?

Instead, she was met with wide eyes, red cheeks, thin lips. Robert looked like he was about to explode. He jerked his eyes to Ethan and looked like he was about to leap over the table.

"A baby?" he finally gritted out. "Harper, you don't know what you're getting yourself into."

Well, that sounded a little…judgmental. Who was he to tell her anything about parenting, considering he hadn't known she was around until she was an adult? Even then, he had seemed to have little interest in playing daddy.

"Harper will be a wonderful mother," Ethan stated, coming to her defense.

Robert shifted his attention between Ethan and Harper. "I'm sure she will, but is she aware that the father of her child is a blackmailing bastard?"

Harper gripped the edge of the table. "Robert. What has gotten into you?" she demanded, stunned at his accusation and outburst.

"I think it's time for us to go." Ethan took her hand and started to come to his feet. "Clearly this was a bad idea."

"Oh, don't go yet," Robert demanded. "I was just getting to the good part."

Harper remained in her seat, her hand in Ethan's as he tried to nudge her up. She stared across the table at her father, waiting for some type of explanation.

"What are you talking about?" she asked.

"Let's go, Harper," Ethan tugged again.

Robert reached across the table and took her other hand. "Listen to what I have to say before you go."

Harper jerked her attention between the two men she was practically torn between. Both radiated anger and rage, and she'd never been more confused.

"Don't listen to him," Ethan pleaded. "Come with me, Harper."

Irritated, she pulled her hands from each of them and glanced around the restaurant. People were starting to stare, and that was the last thing she wanted.

Harper stared up at Ethan. "Sit down."

Robert remained the focus of Ethan. Harper had never seen such fury on anyone, let alone the man she'd fallen for. Nerves and fear pumped through her because whatever was going on had both men angry, and it seemed she was caught in the middle.

How could they already be feuding? They'd just met.

Unless they hadn't... Did they know each other? But they'd acted like strangers before. Was that a lie?

Ethan finally eased back down in his seat and re-took Harper's hand, resting on the arm of her dining chair. But his eyes remained locked across the table.

"What are you talking about...this blackmail?" Harper demanded of her father. "I just introduced you and Ethan."

"Oh, I've known Ethan since he was about twelve." Robert shifted his focus. "Or was it thirteen?"

Harper glanced to Ethan. "Is that true?"

He remained silent, and Harper wasn't sure he was going to say a word, but he finally blinked and turned his attention to her. That rage that had been pouring off him seemed to vanish, replaced by something akin to guilt and remorse in his eyes.

Dread settled heavy in her gut. He'd been lying to her?

"Robert was my stepfather for five years," Ethan ultimately replied.

Those words hung in the air, and Harper attempted to process each one. There was no way this was true. Her biological father was the monster who'd stolen everything from Ethan? The man she wanted to build a relationship with, whose support and approval she'd wanted to gain, was scheming and deceitful?

Harper's breath caught in her throat as she stared back at Ethan. "You used me," she accused.

Ethan shook his head. "Never once," he murmured, his gaze holding hers, almost silently begging her to believe him. "When we met, I had no idea who your father was."

"I don't believe you. The timing is too perfect and you…"

Harper swallowed the lump in her throat and forced herself to keep her emotions under control. He'd admitted he was a jet-setting playboy. He'd discussed how relationships weren't his thing, yet he'd been the one to propose. Baby or no baby, she should've paid attention to that red flag waving around.

But she didn't have all of the information, from either side. She needed, no, *deserved*, to know the full truth before making any rash decisions. She just wasn't sure that she could believe anything she heard right now.

"Oh, now, don't be mad at Ethan," Robert chimed in. "He just wants to blackmail me into giving his resort back. I never stole it, by the way. He was underage and couldn't do anything with it at the time. I had every right to do as I saw fit. Same with the Montana resort, which I let go a few years ago. It's all business."

Ethan fisted his hands and slammed them onto the table. "I'll ruin you," he threatened. "Is that what you want?"

Robert narrowed his eyes. "You would've turned me in anyway," he accused. "And if I'm going down, I'm sure as hell taking you with me."

There were too many threats flying around based on things she knew nothing about. Her head spun, her heart ached and she couldn't stomach sitting at this table another second.

The two men she wanted most in her life had ruined every shred of happiness she'd built up just moments ago. She was sorely tempted to just get up and walk away from them both.

But she had questions and she wanted answers.

"You're turning him in?" she asked. "To the cops, I assume? For what?"

"The feds," Ethan confirmed. "Your father has been laundering money for years, and I'm sure the IRS would find his taxes more than interesting."

Her head started to spin, and her stomach felt queasy. Harper smoothed a hand over her abdomen and closed her eyes to gather her thoughts and will herself not to be sick after hearing all of this.

"What's wrong?" Ethan demanded, sliding his hand over hers. "The baby?"

Before she could answer, the waiter brought back their drinks and a basket of fresh bread, and suddenly Harper wasn't in the mood for food at all. She wanted out of here, but, unfortunately, she was owed the truth and had to wait so she could hear both men.

Granted, they were both probably still lying, but there was too much at stake for her to just storm out of here in a fit.

When the waiter asked about taking their orders, Harper forced a smile and asked for another few minutes.

Once they were alone again, she pushed Ethan's hand away.

"I'm fine," she stated. "Don't touch me."

"Are you seriously having his child?" Robert demanded in a low whisper. Apparently, her bout of queasiness was what it took to make the situation real to him.

"I am," she confirmed, but the idea of a liar being the father of her baby wasn't helping her worries.

How had she been such a bad judge of character?

Was it just because she'd wanted to believe, wanted to cling to the hope and dream of a family? Was that why she'd foolishly thought he cared for her?

"Do you just set out to ruin lives or is that a default setting?" Ethan growled.

Robert curled his hand around his stemless wineglass. "I had no idea she was expecting your baby. That's hardly my fault."

"Would knowing she was pregnant have made a difference?" Ethan demanded. "You ruined my life once. I sure as hell won't let you do it again, and I won't let you touch Harper's or our child's lives."

"I can speak for myself," she ground out, then glanced to Robert. "Did you really do all of those awful things to Ethan and his brother when their mother died?"

"I did what I thought was best," Robert stated with confidence. "I have no regrets."

"Because you don't have a damn soul," Ethan threw out.

Harper had heard enough. Neither man denied lying, neither man apologized to her for being deceitful and she was tired of all the anger and hate surrounding her.

She slid her chair back and came to her feet. "I'm done here."

Ethan and Robert immediately stood, but she held up her hands. "I mean, I'm done here with the two of you. Stay, eat, threaten each other, whatever. Just do it without me."

She didn't wait to see how they reacted or what they would say. She didn't care. Right now all she cared about was getting away from them so she could be alone with her growing concerns and fears.

Harper hated to admit it, but the betrayal from Ethan hurt much worse than that of her father. She didn't know Robert well; they hadn't exactly forged a deep bond.

But Ethan...she'd gone and fallen in love with the man and thought they were going to build a future together. Yes, they'd only known each other a short time, but the things they'd shared were deep and meaningful. Had he lied about everything? Could she believe a word he said anymore?

She didn't want to think that she was naive

enough to fall for nothing more than charm and sex appeal, but apparently that was the reality of the situation.

And now she was bringing an innocent baby into the mix. No matter how this played out with Robert and Ethan, Harper vowed to protect her baby at all costs. She knew what it was like to have a mother who put her own needs ahead of her children, and Harper was determined that she would be everything to her child that she'd needed in her own life.

As Harper made her way toward the private elevators, all she could think of was that she was glad she hadn't told Ethan she loved him. He didn't deserve to know, and he didn't deserve her honesty.

One day she'd find the man she was supposed to build a life with, but Ethan wasn't that man.

Fifteen

Ethan walked out on the disastrous dinner moments after Harper. He hadn't gone after her, though. She needed her space, and anything he said to her at this point would only make her angrier…if she even listened at all. He'd needed his own space to put his thoughts in order and figure out how the hell to fix this mess he'd been thrown into.

He also hadn't stuck around to say any more to Robert. The damage was done, and Robert was well aware of what would happen to him now. Ethan had already sent the text to Dane that he was turning Robert in.

He hadn't contacted his attorney yet. Ethan had pulled up his contact, more than ready to send the text that would set the ball into motion of getting the feds all over Robert. He'd waited years to break this news.

But Harper. At the end of every thought on revenge, he saw her face. Despite Robert being the monster Ethan wanted to destroy, he was still her father. Harper would be even more hurt if Ethan followed through...especially now.

He would have to seriously consider everything and talk to Dane.

This whole scenario was a complete and utter disaster, and all he could think of was how Harper likely felt alone and confused and betrayed.

Ethan hated Robert even more now than ever. He was pure evil, leaving a path of destruction in people's lives with absolutely no remorse. The man was a total bastard to have no emotional outpouring of affection toward his own daughter. Robert had been stunned about the baby, but he'd shown no joy at the news, and he'd never said he was sorry for dropping the bombshell about the blackmail that exploded in Harper's face.

Ethan shot another text off to Dane telling his brother he'd call later and explain everything in more detail and discuss further action.

He wasn't in the mood right now to rehash the evening's explosive events.

Once Ethan had left the table, he'd walked around the grounds until he'd covered every square inch. He saw his mother everywhere he went and would give anything to have her here for advice. There were many times over the years he'd had that very same wish.

Of course, if she were alive, Ethan wouldn't be in this position in the first place. But then he wouldn't have Harper.

There was no way he'd give up without a fight. He needed that woman, that baby…the future he hadn't even known he wanted.

Ethan made his way back into the lobby and down the hall toward the private elevator. He had no idea what to say to Harper, how to make her understand that he wasn't a heartless monster. How did he make her see that he truly cared for her? That he'd come to care for her more than he thought he was ever capable of. He hadn't wanted to develop feelings for her, but she'd made it impossible to ignore that pull.

When the door to his suite opened, Ethan stared straight ahead to the wall of windows and spotted Harper out on the balcony.

His heart pounded faster, harder. She'd come here and not to Robert. Did that mean she wanted to give him a chance to explain the situation?

With a renewed hope, Ethan crossed the spacious penthouse and opened the patio doors. Harper still wore that dress that had rendered him speechless earlier this evening.

Those dark curls had been released from her updo earlier and now those strands danced around her shoulders. He wanted to reach for her, but he didn't dare...not until he knew where they stood now. She might hate him even more now that she'd had some time to think, or she might have decided she didn't even want to hear his defense. But he wasn't leaving until he fought for the life he had within his grasp.

"I had nowhere else to go," Harper stated without turning around.

Her soft words traveled to him on the breeze and pierced his heart. She sounded so lost, so alone.

Ethan made his way to the set of chairs and took a seat across from her. She kept her gaze on the darkness over his shoulder, the sounds of the ocean enveloping them.

"All of my things were moved here, and my suite was given away," she went on. "I'll be sure to find something else tomorrow, but with the resort booked, I didn't have the energy to think of another plan tonight."

Of course. That's why she was here. It had nothing to do with wanting to talk or forgiving him or even being ready to hear his side.

"I'm sorry," he told her.

Now her eyes shot to his, and he didn't know what hurt him more, the pain or the anger glaring back. She'd definitely had time to think, and from the fury radiating from her, things were about to get worse.

"Sorry?" she mocked. "What exactly are you sorry for? That you used me? That you knew who my father was and never once said a word to me? That you thought I was foolish enough to marry you, raise this baby with you and never realize that you were trying to destroy my father? Exactly what part are you sorry about?"

Ethan pulled in a deep breath. "All of it," he admitted. "Except the part about using you. I never did that. Not for one second. If I could have spared you the pain, I would've. I never wanted you caught in the middle."

"Yet here I am," she fired back. "And you're not too sorry or you would've come to me the second you supposedly discovered the truth."

Ethan hated Robert. Damn it, he loathed that man with every fiber in his being.

But he had to admit he was angriest at himself. All of this couldn't be blamed on Robert. He was just the one who put everything into motion.

Ethan's cell chimed in his pocket, but he ignored it. A moment later, it chimed again.

"Better get that," she said with a sneer. "Might be your brother and you can celebrate your win. But please have the decency not to gloat around me."

Ethan's guilt spread. "There's nothing to celebrate."

Harper cocked her head, crossed her legs and smoothed her dress out. "Oh, really? You mean getting this resort, no matter the cost, doesn't merit popping open the champagne?"

He deserved her bitterness, her snark. He deserved so much more, and he was just waiting for the bomb to completely go off.

"Robert hasn't signed the papers," he informed her. "But that's the least of my worries now. I'm worried about you, about us."

Harper laughed and shook her head as she looked back to the starry sky over the ocean. Despite the calm, relaxing atmosphere, the storm enveloping them was raging out of control.

"Us," she muttered. "You say that like there was ever an us to begin with."

"We're engaged."

"We were," she corrected.

His heart sank as she started twisting off the ring he'd given her. When that had gone on her finger, he'd still been thinking of their relationship as brilliant and the best route to hold on to their careers and raise their child together.

But now? Well, now he wanted her to wear it because he liked seeing his mother's ring on Harper's hand. He liked knowing they were going to build a life together...a dynasty.

He foolishly had just started allowing himself to feel something, and now he could only feel pain—

and guilt, since he only had himself to blame for ruining everything.

No, that wasn't true. Robert had done his share, but Ethan should've told Harper the second he discovered the truth. He couldn't blame her for not believing him now. The timing was just too perfect.

Still looking out at the water, Harper extended her arm and held the ring between her finger and thumb.

"Take it," she demanded softly. "I was naive enough to think something would happen between us. I let myself..."

Her voice caught on that last word, and Ethan felt her pain. His heart ached in a way he hadn't known for so long. This was why he kept himself closed off. Feelings and attachments always led to a hurt that couldn't be ignored.

Another reason why he hadn't seen through his plans of turning Robert in.

"I let myself fall for you," she whispered.

Her words were so soft, they were almost lost in the ocean breeze. But he'd heard them, and the raw honesty of her statement shredded his soul.

"I'm not a heartless jerk who took advantage," he stated, needing to plead his case, but not just to make himself look better. He wanted her to truly know he valued her.

"I know exactly how this looks," he went on.

"But I swear to you that I didn't know who you were until a few days ago."

"A few days. Plenty of time for you to tell me, but you chose to deceive and lie and talk me into marriage."

Harper turned her attention back to him, and Ethan forced himself to look at her. He needed to take his penance; he needed to see her pain to drive home exactly how he'd damaged this innocent woman. All she'd wanted was to honor her sister's memory, to build her career, and he'd turned her life inside out.

And they were having a baby. There was no way to dodge that lifetime bond, and he didn't want to. He just hated the thought that they wouldn't be able to raise the child together, the way he'd wanted to. But he'd have to put that dream away now. All he could hope was that at some point, Harper came to see that even though his actions might have shown otherwise, he really did care for her.

Ethan reached out and took the ring, purposely brushing his fingers along hers. Harper snatched her hand back, and he knew in that instant that all was not lost here. She still cared, she still wanted him, but she was angry with herself…angry with him.

"I don't expect you to forgive me right now—"

"Or ever."

He nodded to acknowledge that he was actually listening to her, even if he didn't like what she was saying.

"Maybe once you have some time to think, you'll see where I was coming from," he went on. "More than anything, I need you to see that you weren't just a pawn in this. You were a victim, yes, but by the time I realized you were caught in the middle, there was nothing I could do about it. I swear to you—I wanted to protect you. I thought I could. I'm sorry I failed."

Harper came to her feet and crossed the balcony to the railing. She curled her fingers around the bar and glanced down to her hands.

The smart move would be for Ethan to remain in his seat and give her the space she clearly needed… but he'd already committed the ultimate sin of betrayal, so what if he added gluttony to the list?

He rose and came to stand at her side, ignoring the twinge of pain when she stiffened at his touch.

"No matter what happens, I'll make sure you're paid for your work on the resort," he vowed. "My attorneys will make sure this ends up in my name. It may take time, but I want you to move ahead just like you had planned."

Harper sighed. "I can't even think about that right now—but I don't really have a choice, do I? My team is due next week and I need this project. I've put too much time into it, and the future of Two Sisters is riding on a successful design. The snowball effect Mirage would have on future work is immeasurable."

That's why he wanted her to know he had her back where the resort redesign was concerned. She might be pissed at him for personal reasons, but she still had a career that she loved and wanted to nurture. She had a legacy to continue…one that tied right in with his own.

"I understand your need to do everything to honor your sister," he told her, reaching for her hand and sliding his thumb across the top of her knuckles. "That's just another thing we have in common. I came here to fulfill my mother's wishes. That's all. The only person I ever intended to hurt was Robert."

"My father," she murmured.

At least she hadn't jerked away from his hand, but he still didn't like the empty space on her ring finger.

"He's not a nice man, Harper." Surely she understood that. "You even said that he had been distant and not much of a father figure in your life. When I told you the story of my stepfather, you agreed he should be brought to justice. This is the same man we're talking about."

He stared at her profile, his heart clenching when her eyes glistened with unshed tears. She turned her head in the opposite direction, but Ethan was having none of that.

"Look at me." He reached around and cupped the side of her face, easing her back to focus on him. "Don't hide your feelings from me. I know you're hurting, and I know I caused a lot of that. I'm trying to fix this mess as best as I can."

"I don't think that's possible."

Wayward curls blew around, caressing his hand. He didn't realize how much he craved her touch until now…until he was faced with the possibility of never having it again.

"Anything is possible," he replied.

Then he did the most difficult thing he'd ever done. Ethan released her and took a step back.

"You stay here tonight," he told her. "I'll give you space and time to think."

Her eyes widened as she turned to face him. "Where are you going? There are no more rooms."

Like he'd be able to sleep or relax without her at his side? But the fact that she was concerned for him despite everything was only another added factor on the growing list of reasons he shouldn't just let her go. They both wanted to be together, but the damned outside forces were determined to pull them apart.

Ethan turned and left her on the balcony. The sniff and soft cry as he walked away gutted him. For all the time, the years, the money and everything else he and Dane had put into finding leverage

they could use against Robert, Ethan was starting
to wonder if any of this was worth it.

Because of his revenge quest, he might just lose
the one woman he'd ever allowed himself to care
for since his mother. And if he lost Harper and their
baby, nothing could ever fill that void.

Sixteen

The elevator chimed, echoing through the empty penthouse.

Harper tightened the belt around her robe and set her glass of water on the kitchen island. After Ethan left a couple hours ago, she'd decided she was more than deserving of a nice hot bubble bath. But now that she was done, her problems were still there.

Apparently, Ethan wasn't done talking, or he'd forgotten something. Or maybe he'd just decided it was silly for him to leave when he had nowhere to go. She'd been shocked when he said he'd let her have the entire suite for the night.

First of all, the place was plenty big enough for

both of them, considering it had other rooms: a den, a game room, a designated office. They could make it work. Second, this was his penthouse.

Damn him for being a gentleman and making her so confused. How could she hate him for just wanting to retain the place his mother had wanted him to have? How could she hate him when she'd looked into those dark eyes and seen a pain she'd never seen there before? And how could she hate him when he was the father of her baby?

But she did hate him. She hated him for making her feel, for making her want…for making her see a future that involved a family that she'd always wanted and then showing her that it was all a lie.

How could she turn back now? She settled a hand over her belly and fought back tears. It wasn't as if she could just erase Ethan from her life.

The elevator door slid open, and Harper pulled herself together, but it wasn't Ethan who stepped off.

"How did you get access up here?"

"I still own the place." Robert stepped into the penthouse and glanced around. "Your boyfriend here?"

Harper crossed her arms over her chest and willed herself to remain calm. Getting worked up wasn't good for her or the baby.

Besides, she'd heard Ethan's side, so she should listen to Robert.

Part of her didn't want to. She wanted to hide and ignore any of this was happening. Was that terrible? She was exhausted, and being fed more lies just didn't seem too appealing.

"What do you want?" she asked, ignoring the reference to Ethan.

Robert shifted his eyes back to her and came farther into the penthouse. "This suite is usually reserved for elite guests."

Harper said nothing as her father came closer and finally took a seat on a bar stool like he'd been welcomed in.

"Listen," he began, flattening his hands on the marble countertop. "I wasn't trying to hurt you."

"Funny how nobody was trying to hurt me, yet you both did," she retorted, anger bubbling back up to push ahead of the pain.

Harper reached for her glass of water and curled her hands around the base. The urge to toss the contents in his face seemed cliché, but the desire was there nonetheless.

"I'm aware I haven't been a great father," he went on. "That was something I had never intended on being. I'm too busy traveling and working. I've done what I could since I found out you existed. I gave you this job as an olive branch."

If what Ethan claimed was true, then Robert was busy traveling and breaking the law, but she remained silent and let him keep going.

And the olive branch? Did he really think that this was the way to build a relationship—by throwing money at her? As much as she wanted this project, she would've taken an invite during the holidays or maybe a few days' visit here and there. But he always rushed in their phone calls or emailed…anything to keep his distance and not get too involved.

"But I should warn you," he went on. "Ethan's out to get me at all costs. That includes using you, obviously."

Harper took a drink and weighed her words. "Whatever is going on with Ethan and me is really none of your concern. Did you come here to deliver a real apology or just to warn me away from your enemy? Because I won't be used as the ball you two volley back and forth."

Robert stared at her a minute before shaking his head. "I see he's corrupted you."

"He's done nothing of the sort," she argued. "I don't trust either one of you right now. But I do wonder why you were so cruel to those boys when their mother died."

Robert pursed his lips, and Harper assumed he was working on another lie—or perhaps he was debating whether or not to tell her anything at all.

"I've always been an opportunist," he stated, easing against the back of the stool. "When I married their mother, I thought I could help her run these resorts. I wasn't quite in the financial position I am now, and I needed a leg up."

Harper snorted. "So you took advantage of a single mother."

"Opportunist," he repeated. "When she passed away, I felt it my duty to take over. The boys weren't old enough to run anything. Hell, they were still in high school."

Harper listened to him justify his actions.

"Why did you hire me for this renovation project?" she asked. "I mean, you barely know me. You toss a few hours of your time my way each year. Even though I'm always trying to reach out and forge a relationship. And don't say the olive branch. I don't believe it."

He stared at her another moment and sighed. "My assistant looked over the portfolio you sent, and she said your designs were fresh and new and exactly what Mirage needed. I agreed because you are my daughter."

Harper hated to ask, but she had to know. "Did you even look at what I sent? Do you even care, or were you just going to throw the money at me when I got done?"

"I didn't look at them," he confirmed. "But I trust the judgment of my assistant, otherwise she wouldn't work for me."

Harper's heart sank. She'd already known he hadn't hired her out of affection or a genuine wish to see her succeed in the business that meant so much to her. But now she realized he hadn't even hired her because he thought she was talented or because he loved her ideas. He hadn't even taken the time to look at a few images…images she'd painstakingly poured herself into for each space of this resort. She'd lost sleep, she'd shed tears, all because she wanted everything to be perfect for Robert and his property.

"Get out."

Robert jerked at her command, and she had to admit the steeliness to her tone shocked her, as well.

"You need tougher skin," he replied. "If every little thing hurts your feelings—"

"Little things?" she repeated. "Hurt feelings? You don't know a damn thing about feelings, so don't attempt to lecture me on mine."

When he remained still, she jerked her finger toward the elevator. "Get. Out. We're done here."

Robert's lips thinned. "You won't make it in the business world if you keep those emotions on your sleeve."

"Yeah, well, from the sound of things you're not going to make it much longer, and you've had yours closed off for decades. So I'll take my chances and be human."

He stared another second, and she thought he'd toss out another nasty remark, but he ultimately turned on his heel and got on the elevator.

Once Harper was alone, she took two shaky steps to the nearest bar stool and slid up onto the metal. Crossing her arms on the bar top, he laid her head down and finally wept.

She couldn't hold the pain in any longer. She had no clue what move to make next. She had no clue how she would ever recover from this crushing blow.

All she knew was that her baby would need her to be strong, and Harper vowed to rise up from this setback and be stronger than ever.

And never let another man near her heart again.

"There you are."

Ethan jerked up from the desk in Harper's tiny office. He hadn't realized he'd fallen asleep, but he blinked and focused on the person in the doorway.

"Dane?"

His twin glanced around the room and shook his head. "Rough night?"

Scrubbing his hands over his face, Ethan leaned back in the leather chair and sighed. Rough night didn't cover it. He'd been tortured with his own thoughts, replaying his actions over and over, wondering at what point he could've prevented everything from falling apart, or if that had even been a possibility.

A woman stepped up from behind Dane and offered a sympathetic smile.

"You must be Stella," Ethan stated. "I'd offer you guys a seat, but…"

The office had no spare furniture—it barely had room for this desk.

"Don't worry about it," she said. "Is there something we can get you?"

Ethan's heart ached, but there was nothing anyone could do at this point, so he simply shook his head and focused back on his brother.

Dane wore his typical flannel and jeans, which looked extremely out of place at a tropical resort.

"You do know you're in Southern California, right?" Ethan asked.

"We hopped on my plane and came straight here," Dane growled. "I didn't take time for a wardrobe change because I was worried about my brother."

Ethan hadn't seen Dane in too long, and knowing he'd rushed here to see him during the most difficult time of his life had Ethan feeling so damn thankful. At least there was one relationship he hadn't destroyed completely.

"How did you know where I was?"

"I know my way around here, too," Dane replied. "But I overheard one of the staff members talking to a cleaning lady, and they said there was a man asleep in the back office. I figured it was you or another guy who was kicked out of his room."

Ethan rolled his eyes and pushed away from the

desk to come to his feet. "I'm sorry I'm not making a better impression," he told Stella. "It's been a rough twenty-four hours."

That megawatt smile widened, and he could see how his brother fell so hard.

"No need to apologize," she told him.

Dane crossed his arms over his chest and leaned against the door. "So, where do things stand now?"

Ethan raked a hand through his hair and tried to organize his thoughts. "They stand in a mess."

"I'll put Robert aside for a second," his brother said. "How's Harper?"

Ethan swallowed and refused to be overcome by emotion. He would not break down, damn it. He certainly wouldn't lose it in front of Dane and Stella. He needed to get a grip, hold it together and focus on how to fix this disaster instead of wallowing in self-pity.

"I haven't spoken to her since last night."

Ethan had wanted to stay, he'd wanted to demand she hear him and understand, but he respected her enough to walk away. She was smart, and he could only pray she came to the conclusion that, despite his mistakes, he'd never meant to cause her pain.

"I told her to stay in the penthouse and I'd leave," he added. "There were no rooms, so I ended up here."

"Is she worth fighting for?" Dane asked.

"She's worth everything."

Ethan didn't even have to think of his response. Harper had come into his life like a whirlwind of freshness and had breathed new life into his heart, actually managing to fill that dark void.

"Then why are you down here sulking?" Dane demanded. "Go do something."

"I was giving her some space," Ethan muttered. "She doesn't want to see me right now."

"Then let's go deal with Robert." Dane cursed beneath his breath. "Not that I want to see the old bastard, but he deserves justice."

"You know I completely agree," Ethan replied. "But I haven't pressed on that just yet."

"Because of Harper," Dane guessed.

Ethan swallowed, but that lump of guilt hadn't moved since yesterday. He simply nodded, unable to go into more detail for fear of being too overcome with emotions. He didn't recall the last time he'd been so consumed by so many feelings.

"I'm going to let you two talk," Stella chimed in. "This is such a beautiful resort, and I haven't been to the beach in ages. I'm going to take a walk."

She went up on her toes and kissed Dane's cheek before slipping away. Dane stepped into the office and closed the door, leaning back against it.

"You need to pull yourself together and go talk to Harper," Dane repeated. "She's had all night to think. I know you screwed things up, but hell, I deceived Stella from the beginning and managed to make things work. You have to be honest and throw in a heavy dose of begging."

Ethan had already planned just that. Harper and their baby were worth putting pride aside and fighting for…no matter what he had to do.

"Where's Robert?" Dane asked, his voice hardened now.

"I'm sure he's still in his suite," Ethan stated. "You ready for a family reunion?"

Dane nodded. "The final one."

Seventeen

Harper zipped up her makeup case just as the chime on the elevator sounded through the penthouse. She stilled, her heart beating fast. She'd been trying to get out before Ethan came back, but when she'd gotten up earlier, her morning sickness had hit her full force.

She was getting a late start, but at least her queasiness had subsided somewhat. She didn't have much to gather since her things had just been sent up yesterday. She hadn't exactly unpacked.

Pulling herself together, Harper inhaled and counted to ten to calm her nerves. She'd just stepped from the master suite and into the living area when the elevator door whooshed open.

But her guest wasn't Ethan or even Robert.

"Hello?" she said in greeting to the striking woman who stepped into the penthouse.

"Hi, I'm Stella." The woman took a few steps in, clearly unsure if she should keep walking or remain still. "I'm Dane's fiancée."

Dane. The twin.

Harper clasped her hands together and nodded. They must've come after talking to Ethan.

As much as Harper would've appreciated another woman to talk to, she really wasn't in the mood to confide in a stranger—especially with one who was associated with Ethan…even by default.

"Did Ethan send you up?" Harper asked.

"No. He thinks I'm walking on the beach."

Harper studied the other woman. Long, silky hair. A simple green maxidress with a denim jacket and little booties. She was definitely not dressed for the beach.

"We hopped on Dane's jet as soon as Ethan texted him about the mess here," Stella stated, as if reading Harper's mind. "And there's no rooms available, so the desk graciously held our luggage. I haven't changed yet."

Harper softened and sighed. "I'm sorry. I'm being rude. Come in, please. Have a seat."

"No need to apologize," Stella replied as she moved into the living area. "From what I heard, you've had an explosive couple of days."

Harper followed and took a seat on the sofa. She smoothed her sundress over her thighs and crossed her legs.

Stella sank onto the edge of the opposite sofa and rested her hands on her knees as she tilted her head, her face covered with concern. Clearly she had been filled in on the series of events that had taken place.

"I'm sorry for just coming up here," she started. "But I wanted to give the guys time to talk, and I thought you might need a female sounding board. Of course now that I'm here, I feel a little silly, since we're strangers."

Harper couldn't help but smile at Stella's obvious nerves.

"I'd like to think I know a little of what you're going through, though," she added. "I'm not sure how much you know about how Dane and I met."

Intrigued, Harper rested her arm on the edge of the couch. "I don't know anything other than the fact you two are engaged."

Stella beamed. "We are, but our road to happiness was not easy. The short version is Dane was an ass, but the longer version is, he had his reasons."

"Sounds familiar," Harper muttered.

Stella went on to explain that her father had won Mirage in Montana from Robert a few years ago. When Dane had come to Montana to get it back, he'd known full well who Stella was. He'd deceived her from the start. But then he fell in love, and Harper could see why.

Not only was Stella stunning with her dark skin, inky black hair and adorable accent, she seemed genuinely concerned, which really said something about her character. To come to the aid of a total stranger was something Carmen would've done. Harper felt an instant connection.

"Listen," Stella added. "I'm just saying that the Michaels boys might be a little hardheaded and have tunnel vision when it comes to their goals. Rightfully so, since their mother left this legacy for them."

Harper listened to all the reasons why she shouldn't be so infuriated with Ethan, but that didn't stop the pain from wrapping its talons around her heart and digging in.

"I just can't believe that he had no clue who I was at the start," Harper stated. "The timing…"

"I understand." Stella eased back on the sofa and crossed her leg. "And today is the first time I met Ethan, but I know Dane. First of all, they look so much alike, it's crazy. But second, I know those two boys have fought hard to get where they are. I truly believe Ethan had no ruthless intentions where you're concerned."

Common sense pushed through the pain, and Harper finally admitted to herself that she believed he hadn't approached her because of her father—

but that didn't negate the fact he hadn't come to her when he did find out.

"Listen." Stella came to her feet and held out her hands. "What do you say I find somewhere to change my clothes and we take a walk on the beach or go grab something to eat?"

Harper's stomach rolled a little at the thought. "I'm still not up to the point of eating," she said, patting her stomach.

"Oh, I forgot! This is so exciting." Stella beamed. "I mean, *I* think it's exciting. Are you happy?"

Harper nodded. "I am. Despite everything, I'm really happy."

Stella smoothed her hair behind her ears and pulled in a breath. "Then let's take that walk, you can show me around and we'll talk babies."

"Are you…"

"Oh, no," Stella replied with a laugh. "But I can't wait until Dane and I start our own family."

"I'll call down and have your luggage brought up," Harper suggested. "There are plenty of bedrooms here, and I'm sure Ethan would insist anyway. I'm still in limbo, but you can change here and we can go out for a while."

"Sounds perfect." Stella pursed her lips. "You're redesigning the resort, aren't you?"

Harper nodded. "The design work is pretty much done, and I'm supposed to start the physical renovations next week. I'm not in a work mind-set right now, though."

"Would you be in the mood enough to give me a hint on what your plans are as we walk?" Stella urged.

Harper felt a spark of delight. "I think I could manage that."

"I'll tell Dane the plans."

Which meant he would tell Ethan, but that didn't matter. Harper wasn't asking his permission, and she wasn't going to be involved in the whole family thing now that his brother had arrived.

Harper might just have to go home and wait until her crew arrived. What once was the most important project of her life had been tainted by a dark cloud and had taken a back seat to the turmoil that had become her life.

Dane had waited so long for this moment. To finally come face-to-face with the bastard who had altered his future and stolen what belonged to him and Ethan.

His brother stood at his side at the closed door to Robert's suite. Dane knew the pain Ethan was feeling; he knew the confusion and angst. But Ethan would have to figure out the next steps with Harper on his own. There was only so much advice Dane could give. He would support Ethan no matter what, but that was one battle he'd have to fight alone.

Ethan rang the bell and took a step back.

"He's still just as much of an ass as ever," he muttered.

"Good to know some things never change."

The door swung open, and if Robert was surprised to see them, he didn't show it. The man had gotten pudgier, harsher. Good. Dane took joy in believing life hadn't been perfect and easy for his stepfather.

"I'm not surprised you're both here," Robert stated, blocking the door from letting them in. "I admit, I was hoping you wouldn't be so clichéd as to gang up on me."

"We're not ganging up," Dane offered. "Just letting you know how things are."

Robert crossed his arms over his chest but made no attempt to move or invite them in. Fine by Dane. He wanted this over with so he could put the black mark on his life behind him and move on with Stella and their life of happiness.

"I can't believe you don't have the authorities here yet," Robert scoffed.

"That's up to you," Ethan stated.

Dane fisted his hands at his sides. He wasn't sure what angle Ethan was taking, but Dane would wait this out. Since they were dealing with Harper's father, Ethan had final say on how they worked this. In the end, Robert would always be scum, but Harper and Ethan might be able to find happiness.

"Sign this resort over to me today, and I'll hold on to the damning evidence that would have you fighting for freedom for the rest of your life."

Robert narrowed his gaze at Ethan, then turned to Dane. "And you're just here for moral support? I heard you already got the Montana property."

"Don't worry about my business," Dane replied. "I'm here because Ethan and I are a team."

"Against me."

Dane shrugged and crossed his arms over his chest.

"Do you want to sign the papers or not?" Ethan asked. "Because this window is going to close soon."

"How kind," Robert murmured.

"I'm feeling generous."

Dane admired his brother for not completely going off on Robert—not just for their past, but also for treating the woman he loved so terribly. Their situations weren't so different. Stella's father was a complete jerk who had been using her to get his resort back up and running the way it should be. He'd promised her the entire resort all in her name, but had never intended on following through.

So, yeah, Dane understood just how much self-control Ethan was practicing right now. Dane couldn't stand the sight of Robert—seeing him again just dredged up all those memories of how much that man had destroyed.

Not physically, but emotionally. All those years ago, Dane and Ethan had already begun pulling apart because of the grief of losing their mother, but to have another blow had really blindsided them.

"How do I know you won't turn me in once I sign everything back over to you?" Robert asked, skepticism lacing his tone.

"You don't," Dane chimed in. "It's a risk you'll have to take."

"You're losing time," Ethan stated. "Do you want to sign or not? Either way, you're leaving the resort today. We need your room, and I'm sick of having you here near Harper."

"Don't act like all of this is on me." Robert dropped his hands and shook his head. "Whatever. Take Mirage, but you're paying for the renovations. I'm done with this place—it's not worth the headache."

Dane wasn't so quick to believe him, but he did sound frustrated and over it. Good. The sooner he was gone, the better for all of them.

"You should have the file in your in-box," Ethan replied.

Robert narrowed his gaze. "Awfully sure of yourself, aren't you?"

"I wasn't leaving here until you signed because I didn't want to put the feds on you. That would crush Harper, even more than you've already hurt her. There was no need to pile more on the burden she's already carrying."

"You have until lunch to sign," Dane added. "Ethan's nicer than I am, but I'm calling the authorities in three hours if Ethan doesn't have the final copy back."

Then if anything happened to Robert, that guilt would be off Ethan and onto Dane.

"They'll be signed," Robert grumbled. "I need to get back to Barcelona anyway. I have real work that needs my attention."

"Don't think we won't be keeping our eye on you," Ethan added. "If you cheat anyone out of investments, properties, money, I will not hesitate to make your life a living hell in ways the feds wouldn't dream of."

Robert let out a mock laugh. "You think I'm scared of what you could do to me?"

Ethan took a step toward Robert, and Dane waited, fully expecting to have to pry his brother off.

"Try me," Ethan said in a low, menacing voice. "I promise, you'll regret ever crossing me or my family."

Robert must've seen something in Ethan's eyes, because the older man nodded and took a step back.

"I'll pull up the documents now."

Without another word, he slammed the door, causing Ethan to jerk back. The echoing of the door sounded through the hallway, and Dane glanced each way, thankful nobody was around. Likely, they were all on the beach or still in bed.

"Do you believe him?" Dane asked as they turned toward the elevator.

Ethan nodded. "I do. He's too arrogant to let himself go to jail. If there's a loophole to save his ass, he'll take it."

Dane hoped that was true, for all of their sakes.

"I need to find Harper." Ethan punched the button on the elevator to close the doors. "I don't know what I'm going to say, but I can't stay away."

"She's with Stella right now."

Ethan jerked around. "What?"

Dane held up his hands. "Calm down. It was my idea. I thought Harper could use another woman to talk to, and Stella texted and said they were going to walk around the resort. Harper is showing her around and discussing new designs."

"And me," Ethan muttered, turning back to watch the numbers light up as they passed each floor.

"That goes without saying, but Stella is in your corner."

"She doesn't even know me."

"But she knows me," Dane countered. "Trust me on this. Stella might just tip the scales."

The elevator doors slid open, and Ethan stepped out first. The lobby had only a few people milling about, going in and out of the buffet area for a quick breakfast.

"I think I should change my clothes," Dane stated, glancing down to his attire. "Oh, Harper had our luggage taken to your penthouse."

"Did she now?" Ethan smirked, though it quickly faded. "I do have plenty of room. More if she's leaving."

"Then maybe you should give her a reason to stay."

Eighteen

"You're a difficult woman to track down."

Harper glanced over her shoulder, and Ethan's heart clenched at the sight. She stood on the edge of the shore, the water lapping up over her bare feet. She held a dainty pair of sandals at her side, her other hand gathered up the skirt of her red dress and her curls tossed around in the wind. She was like something from a dream, something he could see, but not touch. Something that could vanish in a flash.

Her dark eyes locked with his a split second before she turned back to stare at the sunset.

"I haven't exactly been hiding," she said as he came to her side.

"I hear you spent some time with Stella."

"She's amazing."

Ethan had talked with Dane and Stella over dinner in the penthouse earlier. He'd hoped Harper would show back up—he'd even ordered enough dinner for four.

"She seems to think I should forgive you," Harper stated after a moment.

Ethan slid his hands into his pockets to keep from reaching for her. He wanted this too much to screw up by being selfish and thinking of his wants first. Harper was everything to him. Not just because of the baby, but because she made him feel so many things he'd never thought possible.

"And what do you think?" he asked.

Ethan studied her profile, trying to capture the proper words to describe the beauty she radiated.

"I don't know what to think," she murmured.

The gentle waves filled the silence, and he waited.

"Did you have my father arrested?"

Ethan pulled in a breath. "No, I didn't."

Harper's gaze shifted to his, her brows rising. "Why? That's all you've wanted."

"That *used* to be all I wanted," he corrected.

Unable to be this close and not touch her, he took a chance and reached for her hand, the one she clutched her skirt with.

The material fell down around her ankles as he raked his thumb over her knuckles.

She trembled.

"After my mother died, I shut down," he started. "Ask Dane. I even closed off from my own twin. I didn't want to feel anything for anyone. I wanted to crawl inside myself and never get hurt again."

Harper's chin quivered, but he kept going. He had her attention—this was the opening and the chance he'd been waiting on…he'd been praying for.

"Then Robert took the main part of my mother's legacy, and I didn't know what to do," he stated. "I know I was too young to run the place myself, but I would've listened to her managers. I would've done anything to make sure nothing severed that bond between my mother and me."

He drew in another shaky breath and squeezed her hand. "You know that I've been wanting revenge on my stepfather, and he deserves to have everything taken from him. But that all changed the second I realized you were his daughter."

"I don't know the man like you do," she supplied. "I met him when I was twenty, and we've had a handful of interactions since then. I believe you about the kind of man he is. What hurts is the fact you didn't tell me the moment you knew."

Ethan nodded in agreement. "I know I hurt you. Harper, you have to believe me. The second I found out, I started trying to find a way to make sure you were not involved in this backlash. I wanted to shield you and our baby from everything ugly about this. I know I should've come to you, but I wanted to handle it myself."

Emotion clogged his throat, and he swallowed back the lump as his eyes began to burn.

"I wasn't able to protect my mother," he choked out. "You're the only other woman I've ever loved, and I needed to make sure you—"

"What did you say?"

Ethan stopped and blinked. "What?"

"You said you loved me," she stated, tears swimming in her eyes.

A swell of warmth spread through him. He hadn't even realized he'd said the word, but now that it was out, he realized that's the exact word he'd been searching for to describe how he felt about Harper.

"Did you mean it?" she asked.

Ethan smiled for the first time in what felt like days. "Yeah, I did. I love you, Harper."

Tears spilled from her eyes, trailing down her cheeks. He released her hand and framed her face, swiping at the moisture with the pads of his thumbs.

"Sorry," she muttered. "People are probably looking."

"Of course they are. Who wouldn't, at the most beautiful woman in the world." Ethan took a step closer until his chest brushed hers. "And who cares? Don't be afraid to show who you are."

"I don't know who I am," she said. "I wanted to be the reckless woman having a heated affair with this hot stranger. Then I wanted to be the woman who was strong and could be a great mother. Then I thought maybe, just maybe, you and I could grow together and perhaps fall in love and raise our child as a family."

"You're all of those women," he told her.

Harper closed her eyes and licked her lips. "No, I'm not," she said, looking back up at him. "I'm the woman who is a poor judge of character."

"No, you aren't." He tipped her head so he could focus on her and she had no choice but to hold his gaze. "You're the woman who is loving, trusting, caring, loyal. You demand those same things in return, which you should. You're not at fault here. But I do love you. I know you might not be ready for that yet, but I'm giving you all the time you need. Just...don't give up on us."

Harper smiled. "I love you, too."

Ethan had never heard sweeter words. He didn't deserve her affection or honest emotions, but that was his Harper. She didn't hide her thoughts or feelings.

"I want to try to make this work," she went on. "I feel like everything was so rushed. Maybe we could take our time, truly get to know each other more and dedicate each day to growing together."

Ethan couldn't hide his smile. "I'd love that."

Harper went up on her toes and wrapped her arms around his neck. "Don't hurt me again."

Smoothing his hands up and down her back, Ethan shook his head. "Never. I promise to always be honest with you, and we can face whatever obstacles the future holds together."

"That's all I ask," she told him. "I hope you don't care I invited your brother and Stella to stay in the penthouse. It wasn't technically mine, so…"

Ethan slid his lips over her mouth then eased back and rested his forehead against hers.

"I want you to share everything with me," he told her. "I can't wait for you to get to know Dane. We're all starting a new chapter."

"Does this mean we'll be going to Montana to visit?"

Ethan shuddered. "Cold weather? Maybe we could go in the summer."

Harper threaded her fingers through his hair and laughed. "I'd love to see it. I've never been there, and I hear it's gorgeous."

"In the summer," he repeated.

"Fine," she conceded. "A summer visit. Should we go back up to the room and visit with our guests?"

Ethan took a step back, took the sandals from her hand and laced his fingers in hers. "Is that what you want?"

Harper smiled and nodded.

They started up the near empty beach. It was getting later in the evening, and most people were at dinner or getting ready for the free entertainment in one of the resort's nightclubs or theater.

"I want that sense of family," she told him. "I feel like I'm getting a second chance at having a sister and the life I've always wanted."

"I'll give you anything you want," he told her as he guided her to the steps leading to the open lobby. "But I have one request."

She stopped and turned to face him. "What's that?"

Ethan slid his hand into his pocket and pulled out the ring. He'd never been so nervous, because he actually wanted this more than anything. He wasn't using the proposal as a ploy or any other reason than the fact he just wanted her in his life forever.

Harper's gaze landed on the ring, and Ethan wasted no time in dropping to one knee. He'd cheated her out of a real proposal before—he wasn't going to do that again. She deserved everything she'd ever dreamed of or desired.

"Harper, will you marry me?" he asked. "Have my children and grow empires with me?"

With tears in her eyes, Harper nodded her head yes and reached for the ring. "I know I said I wanted to take things slow, but I still want to marry you. I just want some time before we say 'I do.'"

Ethan came to his feet and wrapped his arms

around her waist. He lifted her up and smacked a kiss on her lips.

"I don't care how long you want to wait," he told her. "Just say you'll always be mine and forgive me when I do stupid things."

"Done," she told him. "Now let's get upstairs and celebrate with your family."

"*Our* family."

"I like the sound of that."

Ethan covered her mouth with his, wanting to connect to her even more. He'd finally found a love he'd never thought possible with a woman he didn't deserve. She'd forgiven him, and he would never take her for granted again.

Now they were moving on to their new chapter, growing their family.

Seeking justice and revenge wasn't everything in life.

He had all he needed right here in his arms.

* * * * *

*If you enjoyed reading about Ethan and Dane,
try the Rancher's Heirs series, which is also by
USA TODAY bestselling author
Jules Bennett!*

Twin Secrets
Claimed By The Rancher
Taming the Texan

COMING NEXT MONTH FROM

HARLEQUIN® *Desire*

Available October 1, 2019

#2689 TANGLED WITH A TEXAN

Texas Cattleman's Club: Houston • by Yvonne Lindsay

From the first, wealthy rancher Cord Galicia and Detective Zoe Warren create sparks. She's in town to question Cord's friend and neighbor, and he'll have none of it. So he seduces her as a distraction. But his plan is about to backfire...

#2690 BOMBSHELL FOR THE BLACK SHEEP

Southern Secrets • by Janice Maynard

Black sheep heir Hartley Tarleton is back in Charleston to deal with his family's scandals. But a one-night stand with artist Fiona James leads to a little scandal of his own. How will he handle fatherhood—and his irresistible desire for this woman?

#2691 CHRISTMAS SEDUCTION

The Bachelor Pact • by Jessica Lemmon

When Tate Duncan learns his life is a lie, he asks Hayden Green to pose as his fiancée to meet his newfound birth parents. But when real passion takes over, Hayden wonders if it's all just holiday fantasy, or a gift that runs much deeper.

#2692 READY FOR THE RANCHER

Sin City Secrets • by Zuri Day

Rich rancher and CEO Adam Breedlove is all business. But when a chance encounter reconnects him with his best friend's sister, their forbidden chemistry spells trouble. And when their business interests get entangled, the stakes get even higher...

#2693 ONE NIGHT WITH HIS EX

One Night • by Katherine Garbera

Hooking up with an ex is *always* a bad idea. But when it comes to Hadley Everton, Mauricio Velasquez throws reason out the window. The morning after, is past betrayal still too steep a hurdle, or are these exes back on?

#2694 SEDUCTIVE SECRETS

Sweet Tea and Scandal • by Cat Schield

Security entrepreneur Paul Watts knows deception, so when a beautiful stranger charms his hospitalized grandfather, Paul smells trouble. Lia Marsh seems too good to be true. So good, he falls for her himself! Now her secrets could tear them apart—or bind them even closer.

YOU CAN FIND MORE INFORMATION ON UPCOMING HARLEQUIN® TITLES, FREE EXCERPTS AND MORE AT WWW.HARLEQUIN.COM.

HDCNM0919

Get 4 FREE REWARDS!

We'll send you 2 FREE Books <u>plus</u> 2 FREE Mystery Gifts.

Harlequin® Desire books feature heroes who have it all: wealth, status, incredible good looks... everything but the right woman.

FREE Value Over **$20**

SPECIAL EXCERPT FROM

HARLEQUIN
Desire

*Developer Tate Duncan has a family he never knew,
and only the sympathy and sexiness of yoga instructor
Hayden Green offers escape. So he entices her into
spending Christmas with him as he meets his birth
parents…posing as his fiancée! But when they give in to
dangerously real attraction, their ruse—and the secrets
they've been keeping—could implode!*

Read on for a sneak peek of
Christmas Seduction
by Jessica Lemmon.

"I don't believe you want to talk about yoga." She lifted dark, inquisitive eyebrows. "You look like you have something interesting to talk about."

The pull toward her was real and raw—the realest thing he'd felt in a while.

"I didn't plan on talking about it…" he admitted, but she must have heard the ellipsis at the end of that sentence.

She tilted her head, a sage interested in whatever he said next. Wavy dark brown hair surrounded a cherubic heart-shaped face, her deep brown eyes at once tender and inviting. How had he not noticed before? She was *alarmingly* beautiful.

"I'm sorry." Her palm landed on his forearm. "I'm prying. You don't have to say anything."

"There are aspects of my life I was certain of a month and a half ago," he said, idly stroking her hand with his thumb. "I was certain that my parents' names were William and Marion Duncan." He offered a sad smile as Hayden's eyebrows dipped in confusion. "I suppose they technically still are my parents, but they're also not. I'm adopted."

Her plush mouth pulled into a soft frown, but she didn't interrupt.

"I recently learned that the agency—" or more accurately, the kidnappers "—lied about my birth parents. Turns out they're alive. And I have a brother." He paused before clarifying, "A twin brother."

Hayden's lashes fluttered. "Wow."

"Fraternal, but he's a good-looking bastard. I just need... I need..." Dropping his head in his hands, he trailed off, muttering to the floor, "Christ, I have no idea what I need."

He felt the couch shift and dip, and then Hayden's hand was on his back, moving in comforting circles.

"I've had my share of family drama, trust me. But nothing like what you're going through. It's okay for you to feel unsure. Lost."

He faced her. This close, he could smell her soft lavender perfume and see the gold flecks in her dark eyes. He hadn't planned on coming here, or on sitting on her couch and spilling his heart out. He and Hayden were friendly, not friends. But her comforting touch on his back, the way her words seemed to soothe the recently broken part of him...

Maybe what Tate needed was her.

*What will happen when Tate brings Hayden
home for Christmas?*

Find out in Christmas Seduction *by Jessica Lemmon.
Available October 2019 wherever
Harlequin® Desire books and ebooks are sold.*

www.Harlequin.com

Want to give in to temptation with
steamy tales of irresistible desire?

Check out **Harlequin® Presents®,
Harlequin® Desire** and
Harlequin® Kimani™ Romance books!

New books available every month!

CONNECT WITH US AT:

Facebook.com/groups/HarlequinConnection

 Facebook.com/HarlequinBooks

 Twitter.com/HarlequinBooks

 Instagram.com/HarlequinBooks

Pinterest.com/HarlequinBooks

ReaderService.com

**ROMANCE WHEN
YOU NEED IT**

PGENRE2018

Love Harlequin romance?

DISCOVER.

Be the first to find out about promotions, news and exclusive content!

 Facebook.com/HarlequinBooks

 Twitter.com/HarlequinBooks

 Instagram.com/HarlequinBooks

 Pinterest.com/HarlequinBooks

ReaderService.com

EXPLORE.

Sign up for the Harlequin e-newsletter and download a free book from any series at **TryHarlequin.com.**

CONNECT.

Join our Harlequin community to share your thoughts and connect with other romance readers!
Facebook.com/groups/HarlequinConnection

HARLEQUIN®

ROMANCE WHEN YOU NEED IT

HSOCIAL2018

THE WORLD IS BETTER WITH

Romance

Harlequin has everything from contemporary, passionate and heartwarming to suspenseful and inspirational stories.

Whatever your mood,
we have a romance just for you!

Connect with us to find your next great read,
special offers and more.

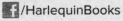 /HarlequinBooks

@HarlequinBooks

www.HarlequinBlog.com

www.Harlequin.com/Newsletters

HARLEQUIN®

A *Romance* FOR EVERY MOOD™

www.Harlequin.com

Reward the book lover in you!

Earn points on your purchase of new Harlequin books from participating retailers.

Turn your points into **FREE BOOKS** of your choice!

Join for FREE today at
www.HarlequinMyRewards.com.

Harlequin My Rewards is a free program (no fees) without any commitments or obligations.

MYR18